THE ONEDIN LINE:
The White Ships

'I am being followed,' she announced to the flickering tongues of flame guttering up the chimney.

James frowned. 'Followed? By whom?'

She turned to face him. I don't know. But wherever I go, whenever I turn my head, something – it – is there. A shadow, slipping away.'

'A what – ?'

The room lay still and quiet, while the rain tapped feverishly against the window-panes like the scrabblings of a dead man's fingers.

'A ghost,' said Elizabeth.

THE ONEDIN LINE:
The White Ships

Cyril Abraham

A STAR BOOK
published by
the Paperback Division of
W. H. ALLEN & Co. Plc

A Star Book
Published in 1986
by the Paperback Division of
W. H. Allen & Co. Plc
44 Hill Street, London W1X 8LB

First published in 1979 by Star Books

Printed and bound in Great Britain by
Anchor Brendon Ltd, Tiptree, Essex

ISBN 0 352 30400 6

By arrangement with BBC Books,
a division of BBC Enterprises Ltd.

For John and Rosemary

Chapter One

They had been bowling along cheerily, running before the S.E. Trades with a sunny sky above and an emerald green sea beneath, when the wind veered sharply, the temperature dropped, and a pampero came spewing out of the south-west. It almost caught them aback but Baines, yawning idly on the poop, caught sight of the tell-tale line squall rapidly massing above the horizon. He brought the ship round on her heels, and by the time James arrived on deck had reduced canvas to three lower topsails and the fore topmast staysail.

'We're in for a blow,' said Baines. He bit off a massive chaw of tobacco, bulged it into his cheek, and waited for the first heavy sea to break aboard.

James clenched a cigar between his teeth, flared a match and cupped his hands. 'Pampero,' he stated. 'It will soon blow itself out.'

That had been three days ago and during that time the pampero had circled them like a ravenous beast cheated of its prey. The wind increased to hurricane force and blew from every point of the compass before steadying from the south-east; mountainous seas thundered aboard and the decks were full of water to the tops of the bulwarks; the fore and main lower topsails carried away and blew out of their bolt ropes; Baines ordered the mizzen lower topsail to be goose-winged and kept the ship's head facing the seas.

The *Esmeralda* bucked and plunged, tossed manes of water over her head and champed angrily at the clawing sea. In revenge the sea carried away the galley doors and the poop skylight, stove in the starboard lifeboats and flooded the saloon and officers' quarters aft. The crew's accommodation forward fared no better; mattresses and bedding were soaked and their gear floated in a surging scum of ice-cold water. There was not a stitch of dry clothing aboard, no warm food to line their stomachs. Then, to add to their misery, it was discovered that salt water had infiltrated into the fresh water tanks.

The wind never abated and slowly its inexorable pressure drove the *Esmeralda* towards the distant shoreline of the Brazilian coast.

Just before noon the sun, breaking through a scud of riven cloud, enabled James and Baines to take the first sight for three days. In the tiny chartroom they spread out the blue-back chart and pored over the plot.

'If this keep up,' said Baines, 'we'll be druv on a lee shore.'

They had been running up the coast, bound from the Plate with a cargo of grain and heading for Santos to top off with coffee. Their present position put them 140 miles south of Santos, tucked snugly beneath the great bulge of northern Brazil, and about 90 miles north of their last hope of refuge, the small port of Paranagua. Between was nothing but a desolation of sea-bound cliffs, sandhills and swamps.

'Inhospitable country,' commented Baines. 'Very inhospitable.'

James was flicking over the pages of the Admiralty Pilot. 'Nothing here,' he said disgustedly and replaced the volume in its rack.

'You could hardly expect it,' said Baines. 'I mean, there's nothing worth the trouble of surveying beyond a few fishing villages and bow-and-arrow Indians.'

James frowned. 'Fishing villages? That means fresh water.'

Baines grunted. 'We got more to worry about than a sup o' water.'

James explained patiently. 'Fresh water means rivers. And rivers flow out to the sea.'

Baines shook his head. 'I know what you are driving at,

but most of 'em are no more than muddy creeks with sand-bars and shallows as soup spoons.'

'We have no choice,' said James testily. 'We find an inlet or pile up during the hours of darkness.'

'We've only about six hours of daylight left,' Baines reminded him.

'Then the sooner we get started the better,' said James. 'Bring her round, Captain Baines.'

Anything was better than waiting for the inevitable. At least they could feel that their fate lay in their own hands.

The yards were squared and the *Esmeralda* stood in to the land. At the end of an hour, with the wind screaming over the quarter, they sighted a low-lying shoreline with a buttress of high cliffs towering in the background. The surf was a long line of curling foam, roaring over sand spits and hurling itself high in a fury of white spume.

'*Very* inhospitable,' commented Baines drily. He put the helm down, braced the yards up sharp, and the *Esmeralda* once again began to claw her way off the coast.

They tacked and wore ship, inching their way northward, scanning the coastline for signs of a tell-tale break in the pounding surf. It was a desperate battle; on each leg they lost ground; big seas, the bellowing wind and the continual shortening of sail was having its effect, gradually setting the *Esmeralda* closer and closer towards the wild and savage shore.

After five hours of exhausting, mind-numbing struggle they had almost lost hope. The land now lay no more than five miles off their port quarter and it was doubtful whether they would have sufficient sea room for another tack.

'Beach her,' said James. It was the only decision left. Together they eyed the thundering surf. Nothing could live in that maelstrom of pounding water. A man would be mashed to pulp long before he could reach the illusory security of dry land. 'We'll abandon ship the moment she strikes,' he added.

'I'll take one last look-see,' said Baines. Slinging the telescope over his shoulder he swung into the mizzen shrouds and clambered aloft like a huge ungainly monkey.

James stuffed his hands in his pockets and watched him go. It was the end, he thought. The end of his dreams. He felt neither fear nor bitterness. Just a general sadness that life could be so short with so much to do. Time seemed to have raced past. Anne's death seemed to be only yesterday, and yet his daughter, Charlotte, would soon be blossoming into young womanhood. He remembered burying Albert at sea. The inconsolable Elizabeth. Daniel Fogarty – that thorn in the flesh – where was he now? Sheep-herding in Australia from all accounts. He thought of brother Robert, parsimonious as ever, nose to the grindstone, but his new-fangled departmental store had succeeded beyond all measure. He thought of old battles. Of his old arch-enemy Callon, now long dead and buried. Of Iron Jack Frazer, his massive frame now crumpled with age. Of Emma, Fogarty's deserted wife, wailing through an empty house like a mad spirit. He thought of the shipping empire he was in the process of creating: one small company, the Onedin Line Limited: a private company capitalised with its original £100 worth of shares, fifteen per cent to Elizabeth and fifteen to Robert. The company sitting, like a voracious spider, at the centre of a web of interlocking subsidiary companies. He wondered how much he was worth. A million? He mentally shrugged. He had never been given to counting in pounds, shillings and pence. Money was a commodity to be put to work like any other. If only Anne had delivered him of a strong son to carry on his name instead of a weakling daughter who, the day she inherited, would no doubt be snapped up by some get-rich-quick ne'er-do-well and the Onedin Line and all his dreams would be as though they had never existed.

James was brought from his reverie by a hail from the mast-head. Baines, feet rooted to the cross-trees, one massive arm locked about the dizzily swaying topmast, mouthed and pointed with his free arm.

The wind tore away his words and tossed them to the raging sea. James followed the direction of the pointing arm, hoisted himself into the mizzen rigging, hooked an arm around the backstay and focused his binoculars upon the shoreline. At first he saw nothing but an unbroken line of surf stretching as far as the eye could see. Then he glimpsed a vague shape with something of the appearance of a hump-backed whale. He blinked his eyes, wiped the binocular lens clear of spray and carefully refocused. The humpback shape resolved itself into a roil of black water on either side of which the enormous rolling breakers mysteriously parted. It could mean only one thing. A deep-water channel, he decided, and scrambled down to the poop.

Baines arrived at the same time. 'It's a inlet,' he crowed. 'Hardly wide enough to spit across, but it will serve, by God!'

James nodded agreement. 'Bear away and crack on all sail. It's our only chance.'

Baines picked up the megaphone. 'All hands! All hands, roust out! Roust out and make sail! Shake out the jib! Stand by sheets and braces!'

The jib rattled up, flapping and bellowing in the wind. The ship's head payed off, the topsails flapped and cracked.

'Main tops'l haul!'

The weather braces were let go. The yards on the main-mast flew around with the weight of the wind as the port watch hauled furiously to take in the slack of the lee braces.

'Main course!'

The exhausted topmen, lying out on the crazily swinging yards, cast off the gaskets. The enormous lower course filled, roared and flailed like a wild thing while the watch floundered waist-deep in icy water as they hauled with all their might on sheets and tacks. The sail bellied and boomed and the *Esmeralda* leaped forward, shouldering aside the storm-wracked sea.

Wearily they set the fore course, hauled around the upper topsail yards, then, as the ship bore down upon the land, sought what shelter they could from the raging seas and howling wind.

The *Esmeralda* heeled and, with green water pouring over her lee rails, ran before the wind until the shoreline loomed no more than a mile distant and the surf roared and thundered like a cannonade.

Steep escarpments stretched north and south. Between a pair of wind-worn buttresses of striated rock the sea boiled in a turbulence of black water, flinging clouds of spray high in the air as it pounded and clawed at the base of the cliffs.

'It's now, or never,' said James. 'Bring her round.'

Baines put the helm over. The weary hands once more tailed on to sheets and braces, the ship's head came round, the yards were squared, and the *Esmeralda* plunged for the centre of the maelstrom.

The following sea rose in mountainous combers that poured through the narrow neck of the inlet in a surging mass of raging water. The ship spun crazily, bobbing and twisting, rudder fighting the helm. She rose stern-first above the crest of each towering wave before plunging headlong down the racing green slopes to bury her nose in a wall of moving water. The bowsprit carried away, hung for a moment like a broken tooth, then was swept away in the turmoil while the jib sail blew out, becoming in an instant a thing of rags and tatters flailing madly at the wind. The deck was a boiling cauldron of foaming water, sluicing around hatches and breaking in thunderous roars against the deck housing. The voice of the wind, funnelling between the twin bastions of eroded rock, rose to a demonic howl while the sea bore the ship onward like a piece of flotsam adrift in a mill-race.

The crew, clinging to stays and shrouds, listened to the snarl of the sea and the banshee wail of the wind and waited fearfully for the bone-jarring shock of the ship's striking. The towering buttresses swept past in a welter of high-flung spray and a storm of spindrift. Then suddenly the gap widened and they found themselves once more on an even keel with the *Esmeralda* skimming across the surface of a wide shallow bay.

'Lee-O!' roared Baines and put the helm down. The *Esmeralda* turned skittishly, her head came up into the wind, the sails backed and she began to make sternway.

'Let go the port anchor! Let go starboard!' bellowed Baines. The chains rattled through the hawse pipes, the *Esmeralda* leaned back and twenty minutes later was bobbing easily at anchor in the lee of the land with sails furled and the wind shouting overhead.

'Break out the rum,' said James. 'I think we've earned it.'

While the cook ladled out tots of the fiery raw spirit, James paced the poop and took stock of his surroundings.

The inlet was a bottleneck through which the sea, driven by the fury of the storm, poured in an angry torrent. The bay swung sharply to the south and rather resembled the shape of a baby's bottle turned on its side. Protected from the sea by a long escarpment of rock and sand it nestled between folds of heavily-wooded hills which rose to a high plateau reaching back to the interior. Here and there the smoke from wood fires curled in the air to be wafted into long blue streamers by the wind. James picked up the binoculars and scanned the shoreline.

He identified a few scattered villages, each no more than a cluster of grass-thatched huts clinging to the water's edge. A few primitive canoes were drawn up upon the beach, out of reach of the wash of the curling breakers. Fishing nets hung from drying poles and a scattering of dark-skinned figures wandered aimlessly about, pausing now and again to gesticulate and stare towards the strange intruder into their private domain.

'Heathen savages,' said Baines. 'I daresay it's the first time they ever sighted a deep-sea craft at close hand.'

'We wish them no harm,' replied James. 'When the weather breaks we'll take a boat ashore and pay them a visit.'

'They are bow-and-arrow Indians,' warned Baines, 'and I doubt they'll take kindly to strangers.'

'They'll trade,' said James confidently. 'Everyone likes to think they are getting something for nothing.'

Baines scratched his head. 'That's exactly what they've got – nothing.'

'Fresh water,' said James. He pointed to a stand of timber. 'And a new bowsprit.'

Overnight the skies cleared and at dawn the sun rose above the escarpment to pour its furnace heat into the bowl of the land-locked bay. The air was still and humid and the *Esmeralda* lay becalmed in a lake of fire. Not a ripple disturbed the surface and the silence was broken only by the harsh cries of distant birds and the unearthly ululations of howler-monkeys. Already a heat haze was making the shoreline shimmer and eddy as though it were no more than a far-off mirage.

Baines mopped his face with a red bandanna. 'Small wonder ships don't make it a port o' call. Land-locked and windbound, not a breath of air and hot enough to fry fritters.'

James nodded agreement. 'Rest the crew and feed 'em up.' He nodded towards the narrow inlet. 'It's going to be a long pull to haul her out.'

'It must be the last place God made,' said Baines. 'Not a mite of use to man nor beast.'

'Oh, I don't know,' said James. He pointed towards half-a-dozen canoes casting their nets close inshore. 'They manage to make a living.'

Baines shrugged. 'Hand-to-mouth existence. No fish, no eat.' He leaned across the poop rail and called down to the Mate, a brawny young man of Viking beard and battered nose. 'Mr Murdoch. We are off ashore for a spell, so keep a sharp look-out for signals.'

'Aye, aye, sir,' replied Murdoch, more than pleased to have the ship to himself for a few hours and for once be free of the watchful eyes of Owner and Captain.

Baines looked up at the furled sails, already bleaching in the sun. 'And, Mr Murdoch, hang out the canvas to dry. Then the hands can have a make-and-mend. Tell the cook, double rations all round, compliments of Mr Onedin.'

'Aye, aye, sir,' Murdoch answered enthusiastically. It was evidently going to be a lazy day, after all.

The boat's crew were ready, the companionway lowered, and James took his place in the sternsheets as Baines took the tiller.

'Back water, starboard,' ordered Baines. 'Give way, port. Give way together.'

The ship's boat, clinker-built and pulling eight oars, swung away from the ship and headed for the nearest village. The oars dipped rhythmically, the blades flashed in the sun and the *Esmeralda* slowly fell astern, her image a dancing reflection in the mirrored surface of the bay.

The carpenter and his mate drowsed peacefully in the bows, the oarsmen, sweat gleaming on their bare torsos, pulled with a will, looking forward to stretching their legs ashore. James tilted his straw sombrero over his eyes and listened to the purl of the water, the creak of the rowlocks and the soporific splish-splash of the oars while the shore neared and took on a sharper outline.

The fishermen, he noticed, had hauled in their nets and were now paddling furiously for the beach. Baines was right, he thought, they were ignorant savages, alarmed at this intrusion into their privacy, and took comfort from the bale of trade goods lying on the bottom boards as well as the holstered pistol at his hip.

They grounded the boat on a stretch of sand lapped by tiny wavelets. The village was deserted. A huddle of dilapidated huts clustered about an open space of bare ground. Clay cooking pots steamed and simmered over smouldering wood fires.

'They're a nervous lot,' said Baines. He dipped his fingers into one of the pots and tasted experimentally. 'Fouler than bilge water. Tastes like fish glue.'

Behind the village stretched a forest of tall trees with rampant vegetation growing between. Giant ferns raised their fronds above a tangle of wild undergrowth reeking of decay. Ropes of liana looped jungle paths for tribes of chattering monkeys. To the north, a little beyond the ring of huts, a wide shallow stream burbled over rock and shale to wind through a cultivated area in which grew rows of stunted corn, yams, and pepper plants.

'Fresh water,' said James. 'We'll strike a bargain with them.' He set down the pack of trade goods and began to unroll and lay out the contents while the carpenter hefted his axe and wandered across to inspect the stand of trees. He selected one, chopped experimentally at the tough bark, and bent to examine the sapwood. There came a *swish* and an arrow thunked into the tree just above his head.

13

The carpenter stared in horror at the quivering arrow, turned and began to run back.

'Walk, don't run,' called James.

Baines strolled towards the tree, passing the white-faced carpenter.

'It was only a warning, Chippy,' he said cheerfully. 'If they'd meant business, you'd have been skewered like a porcupine.' He walked to the tree, tugged out the arrow and carried it back. 'Tipped with iron,' he told James. 'So they must have contact with some sort of civilisation. What do we do now?'

'Sit and wait,' said James.

He spread out half a dozen coloured blankets and an assortment of hand-axes and knives. Then, with Baines at his right hand, the still-shaking carpenter at his left and the boat crew looking nervously over their shoulders, he squatted cross-legged like a huckster in the market place and waited patiently upon events.

Insects murmured drowsily. A large blue butterfly winged its way past to settle upon a parasitic orchid. A man emerged from the trees and began to walk towards them, his hands held wide in the universal gesture of peace.

He was a greybeard, a wizened old man bowed with age. A nut-cracker face peered from under the brim of a wide straw sombrero. He wore a faded serape which reached to his knees and thick puttees wound around his lower legs.

The man halted a few paces before them and, sweeping off his sombrero with grave courtesy, mouthed a few incomprehensible phrases.

James, who could barely comprehend the rounded accents of a southern Englishman, much less a foreign tongue, looked hopefully at Baines. Baines's linguistic abilities never ceased to amaze him. The man seemed to have command of more tongues than heard in the Tower of Babel.

Baines shook his head. 'I can't get the hang of it.' He eyed the man's puttees. 'He's dressed Portugee fashion. I think he's a mestizo – a half-breed.' He addressed the man slowly, in carefully enunciated Portuguese.

The wizened face crinkled and the mouth opened in a

gap-toothed smile. He replied haltingly in the same language, pausing to search for an unfamiliar phrase like someone rummaging through a lumber room of long-forgotten memories.

'He says he is Dom Pedro Ramirez and his chief wants to know why the great flying ship is here, and what do we require, for they are only a poor people,' translated Baines.

'Tell him,' said James. 'That the bad storm blew us in, that we come in peace and wish them no harm, and that in earnest of our good intentions we offer rich presents.'

Baines selected a blanket and a knife, handed them to the spokesman and entered into what appeared to be an exchange of civilities.

Dom Pedro bobbed his gratitude, turned and hallooed back into the forest.

In a few moments the tribe emerged. First came the young men armed with an assortment of fishing spears and bows and arrows. They advanced in a ragged line, shaking their weapons and grimacing furiously while behind them straggled old men, women and children.

'They don't mean no harm,' said Baines. 'So just hold fast. I've seen the same thing many's the time afore, plying out of the Gold Coast. They're only boosting up their courage. Pretending they're not afraid.'

The skirmish line approached to within a few yards, then lowering their weapons, stood scratching themselves and grinning sheepishly until a broad-shouldered man holding a ceremonial spear stepped from their ranks and spoke quickly and gutturally to Ramirez.

The greybeard, radiating self-esteem at the importance of his new-found duty, translated slowly.

'This feller is the headman,' said Baines. 'Near as I can make out his name is Anzuelo and he wants to know why people rich enough to own so magnificent a ship wish to trade with a people as poor as his own?'

'Tell him that we have finished trading, that these are all the goods we have left and that we offer them in friendship. In return we will accept water and a tree.'

Baines embarked upon a lengthy speech, throwing in a few

15

flowery phrases for good measure, at the end of which Anzuelo looked puzzled and cross-questioned his go-between.

'He understands about the water,' said Baines. 'But he wants to know why we require a tree.'

Before replying James addressed himself to the carpenter. 'What did you make of it, Chippy? Was the timber sound?'

'Best Parana pine,' said the carpenter. 'Couldn't wish for anything better.' He extended an arm and encircled the stand of trees. 'You could build an entire fleet of ships out of this lot alone.'

'I'll bear it in mind, Mr Andrews,' said James. He came to his feet. 'The tree is for a spare mast.' He picked up two blankets, two axes and a pair of sheath knives and loaded them into the arms of Anzuelo. 'Tell him that these gifts come from one chief to another and that we will return tomorrow for water and timber.'

They filled half a dozen beakers from the stream, the carpenter selected and marked a tree, then they returned to the boat, leaving the villagers to pick and squabble over the remaining presents.

James, seated in the sternsheets, thoughtfully contemplated the bay and the low ring of foothills reaching back to the plateau. 'It could make a fine natural harbour,' he mused aloud.

Baines, the tiller held easily in a massive paw, snorted dissent. 'All right at a pinch, but the wind that blows you in don't blow you out, and it lies right in the path of the Trades. Besides, it don't lead nowhere.'

'Everywhere leads somewhere,' said James and lapsed into brooding silence.

On returning to the ship he left orders that he was not to be disturbed and shut himself in his cabin where he worked throughout the afternoon and far into the night. He pored over an atlas, read and re-read the Admiralty Pilots, checked on rainfall and prevailing winds, refreshed his memory as to the principal cargoes shipped out of the ports of Santos to the north, and Rio Grande do Sul to the south. At four bells in the middle watch he stowed away his

16

books and papers and took a turn on deck to smoke a contemplative cigar.

The *Esmeralda* slept peacefully at her anchorage. Overhead the bunted sails hung in ghostly folds beneath a great bowl of sky dripping with jewelled stars. The foothills were dark shadows sprinkled with the firefly lights of slumbering cooking fires.

James counted. Each represented a village, and each village must of necessity have its own supply of fresh water. That meant twenty streams flowing steadily down from the plateau which, in its turn, indicated the presence of a large body of water. He slowly paced the deck while the constellations of the Keel and the Sail voyaged across the boundless sky in their never-ending quest for the glittering prize of the Southern Cross.

He took one last satisfying draw upon his cigar and flicked the stub away. The glowing ember arched through the night to be quenched by the gently lapping waters of the bay. James yawned and stretched. Tomorrow he would venture inland and explore the terrain. A shooting star fled across the sky, a golden spark that flared into brief life then died against the greater darkness. To a superstitious man it might have been an omen, but James had seen thousands before and lacked a superstitious bone in his body.

The following morning he rose early and breakfasted heartily. He listened to the creak of block and tackle and the run of the falls as the remaining ship's boat was lowered into the water then, unable to restrain himself longer from the promise of a new day, he gulped down a cup of hot strong coffee and trotted up the companionway on to deck.

The morning was already hot and sultry. Streamers of mist, twisting and turning like banners of shot silk, overhung the waters of the bay. The foothills, purple and gold, rolled back from the water's edge in a series of humpback ridges buttressing the edge of the plateau.

James leaned against the poop rail and idly watched the bustle of activity in the waist of the ship. The carpenter and his mate were lowering their kit of tools into one of the boats already laden with empty water casks. The leading water

17

party, grinning hugely in anticipation of their expedition ashore, were evidently the envy of the shipboard watch as they swarmed down the falls to the cutter bumping gently against the ship's side. Jeremiah Honest, the boatswain, was last to drop into the boat. He took the tiller and cast off, the rowers plied their oars with a will, and the boat crawled away from the *Esmeralda* to disappear into the mists like some strange, ungainly water-insect.

'Everyone is to have their turn ashore, Captain Baines,' said James, loudly enough to be overheard. 'The hands aboard can occupy themselves with washing down the ship.'

Baines nodded approval and reflected that Mr Onedin seemed to be in an uncommonly benevolent mood this morning. He piously prayed that the humour would continue and turned his head to scowl at an inoffensive seaman whistling softly as he went about his work. 'Stow that caterwauling, Jakes,' he ordered gruffly. 'When we require to whistle up a wind we'll let you know.' He hawked and spat over the side. Too much benevolence could be bad for morale.

Half a dozen canoes had paddled out from the beach and were nosing about the ship like a shoal of shy but inquisitive fish.

'No boarders,' said James. 'Else they'll steal everything that isn't nailed down.'

He beckoned the Second Mate, who was engaged in superintending the stowage of the remaining boat. 'Mr Parslow,' he called down from the break of the poop. 'You have but recently obtained your Second Mate's certificate, I understand?'

'Aye, sir,' replied Parslow, rapidly overhauling his conscience for sins of omission or commission.

James smiled affably. 'Then the work I have for you should fall easily within your compass. I want you to take the hand lead and a bucket of tallow and sound the bay for me. Pay particular attention to the nature of any shallows or shoals. Use the ship as a radial point and work your way close inshore.'

'Aye, sir,' acknowledged Mr Parslow unhappily. It promised to be a long and laborious task, and his taskmaster, he knew from experience, was a stickler for accuracy. Parslow also succeeded in looking baffled at the same time. 'Both ship's boats will be in use, sir,' he ventured hesitantly.

'Then use your wits, Mr Parslow,' said James brusquely.

'What Mr Onedin means,' said Baines, 'is take yourself off and hire one of them canoes.'

As Parslow strutted away on his errand James draped a pair of binoculars about his neck, slung a bag of food and a flask of water over his shoulder. 'During my absence you will be good enough to oblige me by making a chart of the bay, Captain Baines.'

Baines watched James disappear down the companion-way to the waiting ship's boat. He sighed heavily. It was going to be a long day.

James splashed ashore to the rhythmic thud of axes and noted with approval that the carpenter and his mate were already at work chopping down a tall, smooth-boled pine. A party of seamen, skylarking in the stream, suddenly busied themselves with their work of filling water casks. Idling villagers stopped their gossiping for a moment to watch the tall, lanky figure of the stranger striding so purposefully through their village.

They watched him take the winding track that led through the forest to the uplands then, as he disappeared into the deep gloom of the trees, they returned to the more interesting topic of whether Maya would accept the present of a steel knife from one of the sailors in return for her favours. She, of course, had quite properly told her husband and that worthy man was in a turmoil of indecision: whether to accept the knife or demand an axe as well. The village was divided in its opinions. Those who were already the owners of axes and knives sided with the possessors of old and unbecoming wives, who took the conservative view that such an action could only upset the status quo and set an unfortunate precedent into the bargain. On the other hand, those with comely wives and daughters took the liberal view that, as the strangers from across the far waters evidently had an unlimited supply of such luxuries, there should be more than enough for all to share. Whatever the outcome, all were agreed that it would make an edifying source of debate for months to come.

The path buried itself in the forest before climbing steeply to skirt the shoulder of a hill. The air was hot and humid, flies were bothersome and tree roots, buried beneath a thick carpet of pine needles, offered ankle-wrenching traps to the unwary. Somewhere to James's right hand frogs croaked monotonously, almost drowning the chuckle of a stream running nearby. A brightly plumed bird rose with a whoop of fear to perch upon an overhead branch, clattering its bill in indignation.

After half an hour of trudging through green gloom the trees thinned out and fell away from the crown of the hill. Dappled sunlight danced through branches sighing and swaying in a gentle breeze. Then, quite suddenly, James emerged on the edge of the plateau.

He paused, removed his wide-brimmed straw hat, and allowed the cooling sea breezes to ruffle his hair and dry the perspiration that ran down his face and soaked his shirt.

From this vantage point he had a panoramic view of the endless blue ocean rolling away to the horizon. The bare wind-swept escarpment enclosed a bay of burnished copper, a vast, green carpet of forest sweeping down to the water's edge, and the *Esmeralda* – a mirrored toy surrounded by miniscule playthings. Fishing canoes from other villages now plagued the ship like a swarm of insects. A ship's boat, loaded to the gunwales, was pulling steadily away from the shore, oars dipping rhythmically, blades flashing in the sun. He identified the figure of Mr Parslow, seated amidships in one of the larger canoes, lazily hauling in the hand lead.

James drank deeply from his water bottle, tilting back his head and allowing the tepid liquid to trickle down his parched throat. Then he corked the bottle and turned to face inland.

To north and south the baked rock of the plateau stretched as far as the eye could see. Cracked and fissured, riven by gullies, weathered by the eroding winds of the sea, it stood bleak and bare, a bulwark against the onrush of the ocean which, long since, had gnawed through its outer defences to form the hidden bay.

To the west, however, the scene changed dramatically. A mile or two away an uneven ragged scar separated the arid wind-blasted plateau from a hinterland of waving grass. Rich and fertile, the uplands rolled away in gentle undulations to lap at a distant range of hills. And beyond the hills, hazy against the diffused blue of the sky, towered the peaks of a range of high mountains which stretched long arms in a protective semicircle about the vast expanse of savannah.

The wind, buffeting the cliff face, playfully propelled James forward. He walked towards the jagged gash and half an hour later he found himself staring down into the depths of a deep canyon through which boiled a muddy river. It was a bow-shaped chasm, at its nearest point no more than about a hundred and fifty yards wide. The wind sighed and keened overhead and from far below came the echoing thunder of the river.

James raised his binoculars to his eyes and tiny black dots in the distance resolved themselves into herds of grazing cattle. He carefully swept the area and identified taller shapes as a small group of horsemen moving slowly towards a clump of trees surrounding the diamond glitter of water. Vaqueros tending cattle, James decided, and returned his attention to an examination of the terrain upon which he was standing. He wandered about, poking his knife into the semi-porous rock strata, peering into fissures and listening to the rush of water forcing its way through the gorge.

Eventually, satisfied with his conclusions, he made his way back to the eastern edge of the plateau and cast an appraising glance over the unruffled waters of the bay before setting off on his return journey. Halfway down he belatedly remembered his lunch, settled his back against a tree and drowsily munched bread and cheese, his brain turning over plans for the future.

On returning to the village he found that the carpenter and his mate had felled the tree, stripped it of branches and bark, and were busily fashioning the trunk into shape. He watched approvingly as the chips flew from their adzes,

21

then sauntered down to the beach and the waiting ship's boat, passing a water party who seemed uncommonly pleased with themselves.

The oarsmen pulled lustily, grinning hugely as at some secret drollery, and within a few minutes he was back aboard ship with Baines proudly presenting his chart of the bay. It was accurate and would serve the purpose, although, for James's taste, Baines tended to be heavy-handed with the pencil. However, recognising that every man required his measure of flattery, he congratulated Baines and inquired politely if everything had been in order during his absence.

'Well,' said Baines, scratching his scalp. 'We've lost three axes and there's been a run on the slop chest. Knives seem to be in great demand of a sudden.'

'Changey-for-changey,' said James knowingly. 'They've probably found a source of supply of native beer.'

'Maybe,' said Baines. 'But they seem uncommon sober.'

James shrugged. 'It's their money and it puts a shilling or two into your pocket.' He took the chart and made his way below after instructing Baines to send Mr Parslow to him the moment that young man returned with his soundings.

Baines watched him go, wondered what devil's plot was hatching in Mr Onedin's brain, gave up the puzzle and turned his attention to the business of the ship and the problem of hauling her out through the heads and then clearing a lee shore.

By sunset the last water cask had been hoisted inboard, the newly-fashioned jib-boom towed back to the ship, sweated up and stowed on deck, the two boats made fast alongside and Mr Parslow had returned hot and thirsty with a notebook filled with soundings.

James uncorked a bottle of white wine cooling in a pail of water, treated himself to one glass and a grateful Mr Parslow to the rest of the bottle.

Left to himself, James meticulously entered soundings and notations on Baines's chart until, after a couple of hours, he had a complete picture of the nature of the sea bed and the contour of the land. At length, satisfied with his work, he locked away the chart and joined Baines and his fellow officers dining in the saloon.

Baines had broached a couple of bottles of apricot-scented Argentinian wine and the evening passed in an air of quiet conviviality which even the presence of their abstemious owner could do little to suppress. James stayed as long as politeness demanded, then bade them goodnight and retired to his bunk to dream of a bustling port choked with shipping while sacks of gold rained from the skies.

He awoke in darkness to the sound of the steady tramp of feet around the capstan head, the steady rattle of the cable through the hawse-pipe and voices raised in the familiar stamp-and-go shanty of *Rolling Home*:

> *Rolling home, rolling home,*
> *Rolling home across the sea,*
> *Bound for dear old England,*
> *And rolling home, my love, to thee.*

James struck a match, lit the small colza oil lamp swinging in its gimbals beside the bunk head and stared in disbelief at the cabin chronometer. He swung himself over the edge of the bunk and slipped his feet into a pair of rope-soled sandals as his mind registered the time as being little more than a few minutes after three.

He pattered up on to deck in his nightshirt to find the ship astir with activity.

'Wind's shifted,' said Baines. 'We've a puff of off-shore breeze and I reckon we should be able to clear the heads under tops'ls. It will save a power of boat-pulling and I shan't be sorry to claw out to sea, I truly hate a lee shore.'

A full moon hung in the sky, bright as a new penny, and beneath its benign gaze James could distinctly pick out the figure of Mr Murdoch, the Mate, superintending the raising of the anchors, of the tousle-headed Second Mate exhorting the panting job watch to greater efforts as they swayed up a new foremast upper topsail, and the burly figure of the bosun urging the remaining hands to put their backs into it as they walked away with the falls, hoisting the boats to the davit heads before swinging them inboard and lashing them down to the chocks.

Baines had evidently roused out all hands and the cook; even so it would be an hour or more before the *Esmeralda* was ready to put to sea. In the meantime James realised his presence would be but a nuisance. Baines was one of the finest seamen afloat and would, quite properly, resent any interference with his command. James, therefore, tactfully took his leave.

'I'll leave the ship to you, Captain Baines, and turn in for an hour or two,' he announced formally, longing to remain on deck.

'That's right, sir, finish your sleep,' replied Baines agreeably, longing to be left alone.

'Goodnight,' said James.

'Goodnight, sir,' said Baines.

James awoke a second time to find the ship heeling steeply, sunlight slanting through the open skylight and painting golden patterns across the oak-panelled bulkhead. He lay for a few moments listening to the rush and purl of water beneath the counter, the familiar creak of blocks and cordage, the steady keening of the wind. Then, resisting the temptation to hurry on deck, he forced himself to wash and shave, pull on a clean white shirt and freshly-laundered duck trousers. He glanced at the chronometer which wanted a few minutes of eight, sniffed the aroma of fresh coffee, and made his way up on to deck.

He expected to find the Second Mate standing the remainder of his watch but instead found the indestructible Baines slowly pacing the poop deck. The giant greeted James with a salute and rubbed a massive paw over the stubble on his chin.

'I sent all that could be spared below for a spot of shuteye,' he announced. 'We cleared the land at around four bells, then I crowded on all the canvas she can bear, laid her off on the port tack and fetched for sea room.' He made it all sound so simple.

James looked astern, at the creaming wake and the blue ridge of the escarpment fast disappearing in the distance.

'I wonder who owns it?' he mused aloud.

Baines shrugged. 'They can keep my share.'

James grinned crookedly. 'Don't be too hasty, or you might live to regret it,' he said enigmatically.

Chapter Two

Iron Jack Frazer slowly lowered himself into his desk chair, wincing as arthritic bones grated in protest and the ever-present cough rose in his chest to set him hawking and spluttering into his handkerchief.

His daughter-in-law, Elizabeth, adjusted the woollen shawl about his shoulders and patted him gently on the back.

'Stop fussing, woman,' he grumbled, purple-visaged. 'I can't abide fuss.'

'Time for your medicine,' said Elizabeth firmly.

His rheumy eyes followed her progress across to the medicine cabinet. He never seemed to be without bottles of this and bottles of that these days. Evil-tasting nostrums and palliatives which seemed to serve no other purpose than put money into the pockets of a succession of quack doctors, each as useless as his predecessor. There was only one cure for old age, he thought grimly, and it wasn't to be found in bottles.

Elizabeth poured a concoction into a medicine glass and swayed across the room towards him. She moved gracefully, tall and supple as a willow and of a heart-stopping beauty that the passage of years had done nothing to diminish.

He tetchily waved away the proffered glass. 'I can manage. I'm not bed-ridden yet.'

'Open your mouth, you old grouchpot,' she commanded cheerfully.

Wheezing for breath, he lacked the strength to argue and obediently swallowed the mixture. It tasted foul, but the laudanum-tinctured syrup soothed his pipes and brought a small measure of relief. He pulled a wry face, took Elizabeth's hand and squeezed it as though he could draw new life from the cool compass of her fingers.

'We've had us differences, you and I,' he said. 'But we've had us sorrows, too.'

She patted the gnarled old hand. 'Let the past bury the past.' She smiled affectionately down at him. 'We are born survivors, the pair of us.'

He nodded gravely, his mind lost in the cobwebbed memories of the old. 'They've all gone. There's nobbut a soul left but you.'

'Nonsense,' Elizabeth replied briskly. 'You still have three daughters.'

'Comfortably off. Married with husbands and childer to care for.' He sighed. 'It's their bounden duty, I've no right to expect else.'

'You also have a grandson,' Elizabeth reminded him.

The craggy face brightened. 'True. Young William is a chip off the old block. Good blood in his veins.'

She felt a twinge of conscience. Although the boy had inherited her fine bones the cast of features was a daily betrayal of Daniel's swarthy countenance. The same brown monkey-eyes, unruly dark hair and strong jawline; so unlike Albert's fair hair, blue eyes and pale features that she was constantly surprised that no one had ever remarked upon it. In fact old Mr Frazer seemed to take it as a form of compliment. 'The lad's a throw-back!' he had once crowed when William was but a babe in swaddling clothes, 'A true Frazer. Takes after his grandad, don't you, lad?', and had added in jovial undertones, 'Albert's the only fair-headed one out of the bunch. Don't know where he gets it from – unless it's his mother – the Carlins always were a milk-and-water lot with ideas above their station.'

From that moment forward Elizabeth had never lost an opportunity of encouraging the old man's illusions by constantly reiterating: 'He looks more like you every day, Grandfather,' or, coquettishly: 'I know from which side of the family William inherits his good looks.'

'Trouble is, he's nobbut a stripling,' pronounced Frazer, breaking into her thoughts.

'What?'

'William. Young in years but growing fast. You made a mistake in packing him off aboard that damned school ship.'

'The *Conway*.'

It had long been a bone of contention between them. H.M.S. *Conway*, one of the last of the wooden walls of England, lay across the river at her moorings off Rock Ferry, her function to turn a rabble of snot-nosed schoolboys into officers and gentlemen.

'He's no bent for it,' growled the old man. 'He's a square peg in a round hole if ever I saw one.'

'They teach discipline and self-reliance as well as tuition in seamanship and navigation,' replied Elizabeth, quoting from the prospectus.

'Discipline and self-reliance, indeed!' He cocked a shrewd eye towards her. 'If it's a surrogate father you are seeking, you'll need to look further afield than a floating boarding school.'

'Nothing of the sort,' said Elizabeth tartly as an image of Daniel flickered across her memory. 'I am simply determined that William should have practical experience in the business of shipping. Two years on the *Conway* and a couple of years at sea should be the making of him.'

'The practical *business* of shipping is learned here.' Frazer tapped the desk. 'Here, in the office. In the counting house. He's a good head for figures, has young William. He'll be wasted at sea, and you will both live to regret it.'

'He looks very smart in his uniform,' said Elizabeth with feminine illogicality.

'Bucko ships, with bucko mates. That's no life for the son of a Frazer. Albert had the best schooling money could buy. I saw to that. He was a gentleman to his fingertips.'

'I know,' said Elizabeth softly. 'He was the kindest-hearted man ever.'

'A father, that's what the boy needs. Have you ever given thought to marrying again? You have the looks and you are still young enough to take your pick of the best.'

The best? The best was far off in Australia. Elizabeth's eyes clouded with dreams. Daniel. Dear Daniel. Halcyon days misted by time. Idyllic days spent cruising the Azores until James caught up with them and broke Daniel like a stick. She would never forgive him, ever. Dear Daniel. Never a match for the ruthless James, he had sailed away, promising to return and swearing revenge.

She came out of her reverie and playfully rumpled the old man's thinning hair. 'Don't worry, you old grouch, I shall always be on hand to take care of you.'

'I'm not senile yet, not by a long chalk,' he growled, secretly pleased at her decision. 'Now leave me be, I have work to do.'

'You should be thinking of retirement while you still have time to enjoy the fruits of your labours,' she told him.

'Retire?' He shook his head. 'I've worn this harness too long to cast it aside now.'

Elizabeth shrugged. It was his life, and the only one he knew. But of late she had been quietly shouldering some of the burden.

'By the by,' she said lightly. 'I have already instructed Dunwoody to see to it that the *Saratoga* sails on the evening tide.'

'The devil you have!'

He had a sly look about him. The old rogue, she thought. All this time he has been quietly slipping the reins in my hands, and myself thinking I was such a clever-boots.

Of late he seemed to have acquired the gift of reading her thoughts. 'Promise me,' he said, 'that the Frazer Line will always remain family.'

She immediately understood the drift of his reasoning. 'I promise,' she said.

'It will be a long struggle and a hard one,' he warned. 'Folks don't take kindly to petticoat rule.'

'I'll manage. But you have many a long year left to you yet.'

He shook his head. 'The winter will see me off. You'd best send for the lad, I'd like to have a word whilst I still have my faculties.' Another bout of coughing shook his shrunken frame.

'I'll fetch him, myself,' she promised.

Elizabeth crossed by a ferryboat, all thrashing paddles and fulminating clouds of smoke.

At the Rock Ferry landing stage she imperiously rang the bell that summoned the cutter from the training ship lying at her moorings a few cable-lengths off.

H.M.S. *Conway* was a relic of the past and it was difficult to believe that she had last seen active service no more than thirteen years ago. Bluff-bowed, as round-bellied as a hog, she rode high out of the water. Elaborate, glass-windowed stern-galleries overhung the massive rudder and two broad white stripes, running from stem to stern, revealed the square frames of open gun-ports. Her topgallant yards were crossed and a swarm of boys were racing aloft as though pursued by the devil himself. They clambered over the futtock-shrouds, and strung themselves out along lower and upper yards to perform complicated exercises at the commands of an unseen, hoarse-voiced instructor on the deck far below.

The ferryboat gave a blast upon its whistle and churned its way back across river to the distant Liverpool Landing Stage. From Laird's Yards, further down river, came the ring of hammers and the chunner of a steam crane. Up river, a deep-laden barque bore away beneath a cloud of white canvas. The wind picked up fragments of the shrill piping of a boatswain's whistle and a minute or two later a ten-oared cutter rounded the training ship's stern and headed for the landing place at the base of the stone jetty.

The coxswain had a face cratered with acne and could not have been a month older than fifteen. He wore a brass-buttoned reefer jacket with a thin gold band around each sleeve and a cheese-cutter cap perched at the back of his head. The muddy waters of the river slapped at the slimy green stonework as he brought the boat smartly alongside. The rowers tossed oars and Elizabeth, taking the proffered hand, stepped gingerly into the sternsheets and seated herself upon one of the canvas-covered cushions.

At an order from the coxswain the oars were lowered, the cutter fended off from the quay, and the youthful rowers, pulling like galley slaves, sent the boat on a wide, inshore sweep to avoid the stronger currents of the ebb tide which, in full spate, poured down river in a restless brown flood.

Wavelets lapped at the gunwales and an occasional shower of spray, bursting over the bows, drenched the leading oars in an icy rain; a fact which, Elizabeth noticed, far from discommoding them, only succeeded in spurring them to greater efforts. Facing directly upon the straining bodies pulling so manfully at the oars, she became aware of the array of young fresh faces swaying before her. They are but children, she thought, hardly old enough to be breeched, much less put to man's work. She turned her head away and looked towards the ship.

They didn't seem to have made much headway and yet it seemed unaccountably nearer, now looming out of the water until she found herself gazing up at the towering side of a monstrous floating castle. Rows of open gun-ports stared blankly at the nearby shoreline. The bilges were green with weeds that threw out long tentacles like the hair of the drowned. A companion ladder, its platform awash in the run of the tide, climbed steeply up the ship's side to an entry port opening upon the lower deck.

The pimple-faced coxswain leaned against the tiller and with the ease of long practice brought the cutter to lay its stern gently alongside the foot of the gangway. A whey-faced youth with a head like an outsize melon trotted down the ladder and, eyes goggling at the sight of young Frazer's mother, stretched out a helping hand.

Elizabeth treated the coxswain to a heart-warming smile, thanked him prettily and, remembering William's injunctions, tipped him half-a-crown. Then, waiting for the lift of the cutter's stern, she stepped lightly on to the platform grating and, followed by the doting melon-head, mounted the companion ladder.

Although no stranger to ships and shipping, the moment Elizabeth stepped through the entry port she found herself in a world that reeked of distant battles, of the thunder of ancient cannon; a world which must have been familiar to Grandfather Webster, now mouldering in his grave beside Widow Malloy. Massive beams at head-bumping height straddled the fifty-foot breadth of the ship. She had been stripped of armament but the open gun-ports let in a flood of light and a cold breeze redolent of the musky odours of the sea. The shipside was painted an ochrous yellow and ribs as thick as tree trunks reached to the deck above.

Elizabeth ducked her head beneath the blocks and falls that supported the ship's boats and allowed herself to be guided by a stern-faced duty officer up a short companion-way to the deck above. From behind a canvas screen a bee-like drone and a teacher's voice raised in exposition of the intricacies of navigation indicated that the pupils were busy at their schooling, and Elizabeth had time to wonder whether William were among their number or was one of the less fortunate she had seen industriously scrubbing and polishing on the lower deck. Poor William, she thought with a prickle of conscience, she seemed to have condemned him to a Spartan existence of danger and drudgery.

The officer tapped discreetly upon a door set into an after bulkhead, pushed it open and ushered Elizabeth into a co-mingling of two worlds.

The great cabin was light and airy, although lacking in head-room. The stern windows, set in ornately carved embrasures, overlooked the busy Mersey and gave out upon an open gallery running the breadth of the square-cut stern. It was in such a cabin that Nelson must have made his dispositions before Trafalgar and it would, no doubt, have been furnished with the elegance of the age. The present occupant, however, had seen fit to encumber all available space with pieces of solid respectability. A Turkey carpet covered the deck; a blackened-oak desk of Brobdingnagian proportions dominated the room; behind it a high-backed chair of towering Gothic pinnacles, its arms carved into a simulation of crouching lions, blocked golden rectangles of afternoon sunlight pouring through the window panes. A pedestal sideboard of carved oak squatted against one bulkhead as though guarding a private cave from intruders; a leather sofa idled its time beside a circular bookcase. A stuffed owl in a glass case stared unwinkingly at a gull preening its wings on the balcony rail outside. A Zulu shield and a bundle of assegais stood against one corner, and Chinese and Japanese water-colours flanked a large photographic likeness of the Queen. The wind haw-hawed through the chimney of a fireplace fronted by an embroidered screen as a figure rose from the shadowed recess of the chair and came forward to greet her.

Elizabeth produced a smile that would have stopped the heart of a misogynist and extended a hand. 'Captain Franklin?'

He was a tall, angular man of mutton chop whiskers and hooked nose. He wore the uniform of a naval Captain and walked with the lopsided roll of a man long familiar with the heaving of a ship's deck.

'Mrs Frazer? Your servant, ma'am.'

'I am obliged to you, sir, for the favour of your confidence at such short notice,' said Elizabeth, wishing to get the business settled as quickly as possible.

Flaunting her beauty like a banner she allowed herself to be settled in a comfortable overstuffed armchair, accepted a glass of sherry wine and came to the point without further preliminaries. Painting an exaggerated picture of her father-in-law lying on his death-bed *in extremis* and begging to see his grandson, she announced the purpose of her visit.

'I must ask that William be allowed to return with me, Captain Franklin.' To add emphasis she dabbed at her eyes with a wisp of cambric handkerchief.

Franklin tut-tutted sympathetically. 'I see no difficulty, Mrs Frazer. Certainly the boy may be granted a few days' leave.'

'More than a few days, I am afraid,' she said. 'It is his grandfather's wish that he be inducted into the business without delay.'

Franklin frowned. 'Is it my understanding, Mrs Frazer, that it is your wish to remove the boy permanently? In mid-term? Before the completion of his studies?'

Elizabeth had prepared herself for opposition. 'That is so,'

33

she said firmly, adding by way of a sop, 'I am sure that William could not have received better preparation for entering the business of shipping, and I am equally sure that he will in later years remember his time aboard with considerable affection.'

Franklin permitted himself an ironic smile. 'It is only in recollection that schooldays are the happiest days of our lives.'

Elizabeth, who had completed her academic life at the age of twelve, nodded agreement, at the same time noticing a flicker of interest in Franklin's eyes. Evidently the veiled promise had been noted. The goodwill of a future shipowner would be an undoubted asset for the *Conway*'s Captain, who numbered among his duties the unenviable task of recommending his pimple-faced charges as promising officer material to local shipping companies.

Franklin shrugged his shoulders and spread his hands wide. 'The decision rests with you, Mrs Frazer.'

'No,' said Elizabeth. 'It rests with William. Shall we send for him?'

William arrived clothed in a rough shirt of coarse-woven flannel and wide bell-bottomed trousers, with his square-peaked cap tucked beneath one arm. Pigeon-chested and sullen-faced, he stood stiffly to attention with but a sidelong glance towards his mother.

'Sit down, Frazer.'

It came more as a command than an invitation and William obediently perched himself rigidly on the edge of a stiff-backed chair. Gangling and gawky, with clumsy hands and feet, he was, Elizabeth thought dotingly, growing into a most handsome boy. He had, it was true, a somewhat irritable mouth, and hooded eyes which successfully hid his thoughts from an inquiring world, but he also had a firm set to his shoulders and something of his father's stubbornness in the line of his jaw.

He listened impassively to Elizabeth's exposition and then nodded agreement. 'I like Grandfather Frazer,' he said simply, as though that were sufficient explanation in itself.

34

Franklin shook hands. 'We shall be sorry to lose you, Frazer,' he said insincerely, and privately consigning the boy to the devil. Young Frazer had always been something of a misfit, a quiet, self-contained, unsociable lad. Aloof and disdainful of the rough humours of his fellows, he had accepted the usual bully-ragging and chivvying without complaint, had applied himself to his studies with single-minded concentration, and passed his end-of-term exams with contemptuous ease. Nevertheless he was as out of place in the hurly-burly of shipboard life as a fish out of water. Snake-eyes, the boys called him, and there was something snake-like about his personality – an inner dangerous still-ness as though awaiting the moment to strike.

Franklin remembered the Clements incident. Clements was captain of a foretop and had an evil reputation as a sadistic bully. One day he had beaten young Frazer un-mercifully. The lad had never uttered so much as a whimper, but one night six weeks later, Clements had been found unconscious on the upper deck. He had been knocked out by a blow on the head and the calf of his right leg had been deliberately laid open with a knife. Clements had made many enemies and the identity of his assailant had never been discovered, but from that time forward young Frazer had been left unmolested.

Franklin looked at the boy standing still and quiet before him, met a flat unblinking stare from the lidded eyes that reinforced his conclusion that the boy would never com-mand a ship; there was something lacking; a quality of leadership; men would obey, but never follow.

'Change into your shore-rig, Frazer, and report at the gangway,' he commanded, and imagined he saw a hint of amused triumph in the depths of the brown eyes.

Elizabeth and Franklin passed the time in desultory small-talk, then Franklin escorted her to the head of the gangway and the waiting William.

He looked very smart in his midshipman's uniform of brass-buttoned reefer jacket and navy-blue trousers. Quite the little man, thought Elizabeth, looking beyond his years to the image of dear Daniel. Had she been more perceptive she might have realised that William stood alone, with no friends to bid him farewell.

The same cutter crew took them back to the shore, and William silently guided his mother up the narrow stone steps of the jetty. She linked his arm and they made their way to the pier and along the wooden boardwalk to the waiting ferryboat.

As they crossed the Mersey with the paddles ploughing twin furrows in their wake and gulls wheeling balefully overhead, William spared not a backward glance and offered but one comment.

'I hate the sea,' he announced with sudden vehemence. 'I hate it.'

Chapter Three

Charlotte Onedin lay on the floor, kicking her heels and screaming at the top of her voice. Miss Gaunt, her governess, looked up from her sewing. 'Kick and scream all you will, little Miss Tantrum, but your voice will wear out long before my patience.'

Charlotte's shrieks diminished to a wail, then she sat up. 'I want my tea,' she demanded, storm-faced.

'Then want must be your master,' said Miss Gaunt placidly.

'I'll scream, and scream, and scream,' warned the child.

'Dear me,' said Miss Gaunt. 'In that case I'd better stuff cotton wool in my ears.'

Charlotte eyed her new tyrant fretfully. 'When Papa returns I shall tell him that you have been cruel to me and he will send you packing like all the others.'

'Mm,' said Miss Gaunt absently and continued with her sewing.

She was a thin, angular woman with pointed features and fine dark eyes which had seen more than their share of the miseries of the world. Her father, a gentleman farmer, had broken his neck riding to hounds. Her mother had inherited a millstone of debt and quickly followed him to the grave, leaving their only child, Letitia, to the care of an orphanage: a grim fortress where the half-starved inmates served their time in an atmosphere of oppression and harsh discipline. Young Letitia's day of freedom came when, at the age of fifteen, she was farmed out as household drudge to the malcontent family of an impoverished curate.

Twelve months later she sought and found employment as nursemaid to the unruly offspring of a moderately well-to-do haberdasher. A succession of menial occupations followed: seamstress; milliner; under-parlourmaid; upper-housemaid; and housekeeper-cum-cook to a crusty octogenarian bachelor, who gave her a fulsome letter of recommendation before suffering a brain-storm, brought on by an over-indulgence in port wine.

She next applied for the post of governess to the twin sons and younger daughter of Sir George and Lady Lacebury, who occupied an imposing Tudor manor-house in the heart of Cheshire. She had enclosed her late employer's testimonial, added one or two forged references of her own, and been accepted without demur. It was the one deception of her life and troubled her conscience until her dying day.

Lacebury had proved to be a kindly employer. A hearty robust man and surprisingly bookish for a country squire. Time had passed all too quickly as the children grew into young striplings and outgrew the need for a governess.

That, she soon discovered, was the problem with her new occupation; no sooner had she settled in and established control over her charges than she would be off again, seeking a new post.

This, of itself, was a factor which brought two further problems in its wake: as a governess she tended to live a lonely and isolated life with few opportunities of making friends; she also found herself in competition with other members of her calling – rather genteel ladies, untrained gentlewomen whose family fortunes had collapsed leaving the unfortunate creatures with no other means of support. These ladies, having a certain *cachet* and social standing, always seemed to be in great demand, whereas Miss Gaunt, in addition to her background, had to contend with the shortcomings of a broad Lancashire accent of which she had never quite succeeded in ridding herself.

The work, too, was underpaid, most employers considering roof and board, plus the privilege of taking her meals in lonely state, to be reward enough. The result was that, save as she would, Miss Gaunt often found herself living frugally and counting her coppers as she awaited a reply to her latest applications.

Such had been the case when she replied to an advertisement in the *Liverpool Mercury*, offering the post of guide and mentor to the only child of a gentleman of means. She had presented herself at the appointed time to discover that she was but one of a number of aspirants, one of whom was leaving in a state of some tetchiness as Miss Gaunt arrived.

'I sent that other one off with a flea in her ear,' her prospective employer announced without preamble. 'She'd more airs and graces than a duchess.' He had glanced indifferently at her letters of recommendation, tossed them aside, and instead had asked a number of probing questions. They seemed to have elicited satisfactory responses for he had nodded slowly as though communing with an inner self. 'You'll do,' he had said briefly, and she had taken her place in the household, fitting like a cog into a piece of well-oiled machinery.

That had been over twelve months ago and she had soon learned not to be the first to venture an opinion when sitting at table with her uncommunicative employer. She found him to be a morose man of flinty exterior and hard pebble eyes through which he viewed the surrounding world with cold hostility.

'He's still sorrowing over the loss of his wife,' Mrs Gibson, the buxom housekeeper, told her one day. 'He took it hard, very hard.'

Mrs Gibson ruled over a small but contented staff, consisting of Mrs Fletcher, the cook, a sturdy lady who made a fetish of cleanliness; Jenny, the clumsy, but willing, kitchenmaid; Polly and Dolly, two giggling housemaids, as alike as two peas in a pod; and John, the coachman and general handyman, as taciturn as his master.

'That's her, the late Mrs Onedin, poor soul.' Mrs Gibson had indicated a large oil painting overhanging the sitting room fireplace. It portrayed a lady wearing a high-collared dark green dress. She was leaning slightly forward and her lips were parted as though about to speak. The hair was

39

pulled back severely to reveal a sharp, bony countenance with dark questing eyes which, in some uncanny fashion, seemed to follow Miss Gaunt about the room.

'Died giving birth to little Charlotte,' added Mrs Gibson. 'They were very attached, him and her. They were married when he didn't have two brass farthings to rub together. But she stuck to him through thick and thin.'

Miss Gaunt had met the searching gaze emanating from the portrait and shivered. 'She must have been a remarkable woman,' she ventured.

'We shall not see her like again,' Mrs Gibson had stated firmly and closed the conversation.

Charlotte had proved an awkward handful: her sudden outbursts of hysterical rage and bouts of wilful disobedience had tapped even Miss Gaunt's considerable reservoirs of patience to the limit. It had become a battle of wills with Miss Gaunt, armoured by experience, in the ascendancy. Though her hand often itched to give the noisome brat a sound smacking, she had resisted the urge and instead had set herself the task of spinning a web of affection about the child. It had been an unenviable task, but one which, only two days ago, had seemed to bear fruit when she had received the one and only Valentine card of her life. It had been addressed in Charlotte's unmistakable looping scrawl, and bore the printed motto:

> *Someone near,*
> *Someone dear,*
> *Thinks of you this day.*

The problem, Miss Gaunt thought, bent over her sewing, was that almost from the day of her birth Charlotte had been passed from relative to relative like an unwanted parcel. She was treated with indifference by a father to whom she was a constant reminder of her mother's death, and of late she had been subjected to the varying temperaments of a series of governesses. Of these ladies, one had been tipsy throughout the afternoon; another had given the child nightmares with the telling of bedtime stories of ghosts and ghouls, and threatening visits from Old Raw-head and Bloody-bones if she so much as stirred in the night; a third had been a mouse-like creature, afraid of her own shadow, who had quickly given place to a formidable dragon imbued with the belief that children should rarely be seen and seldom heard.

Miss Gaunt stole a glance towards Charlotte, who was now sitting cross-legged before the fire and combing out the plaits of her ginger-coloured hair. She was an immature twelve-year-old with splay feet, awkward elbows, pale, freckled skin, sullen features, and sly eyes puffed from recent crying.

'When the clock chimes six,' said Miss Gaunt, in the tone of one who had given the matter considerable thought, 'we might have toasted muffins, *if* I could find someone, not a thousand miles from here, who would oblige me by fetching the toasting forks.'

The portrait looked down approvingly as Charlotte and Miss Gaunt knelt before the fire and the muffins slowly changed colour to a rich golden brown. They ate them smothered in butter and layered with honey, the mixture dribbling unheeded down their chins, and the fire baking their faces brick red. They drank strong India tea from delicate cups of china served on silver from Mexico, while the gas jets burbled quietly in their tiny globular worlds and the night enfolded the house in darkness.

Miss Gaunt felt calm and at peace with the world. It was a most comfortable situation, one which she felt an increasing reluctance to leave. The house was furnished with an eye to comfort rather than style and the rooms, without being bare, lacked the over-furnished clutter of the more fashion-conscious families with whom she had stayed. The sitting room contained a couple of wing-backed armchairs of the type more usually found in gentlemen's clubs; a rectangular table of mahogany, polished until it glowed; a glass-fronted bookcase loaded with the dullest volumes Miss Gaunt had ever set eyes upon, and from the nature of their contents it was all too evident that her employer was not of a literary turn of mind, since all seemed to deal with one aspect or another of the shipping industry – there were musty-looking volumes of maritime law, of marine in-

41

surance, of navigation, of ship construction, of tonnage rates, and a dog-eared copy of the Merchant Shipping Acts. All in all there was a singular lack of works of either prose or of a poetical nature. It was, in Miss Gaunt's opinion, an entirely masculine room, with a place for everything, and everything in its place. The room of a tidy man of tidy habits.

Sometimes, in her dreamier moments, crook-backed over her sewing, Miss Gaunt allowed her imagination free rein and mentally catalogued the changes she would make if ever she were mistress of such a house. There would be chintz and cretonne, and a silver centre-piece to stand upon the table. Deep green velvet curtains to replace the sombre brown, and an omnium arrayed with a pleasing collection of knick-knacks and fripperies. Above all she would rid herself of the portrait of that devil-woman with the haunting eyes.

She glanced across at Charlotte who, propped upon one elbow, was idly swilling the dregs of tea around her teacup.

'Five minutes more, young lady, then it is up the wooden hill and off to the land of Nod.'

Charlotte, time-wasting, held out her cup. 'Tell my fortune,' she commanded.

Miss Gaunt took the cup, upturned it over the slop bowl, and solemnly inspected the tea leaves.

'I see a young female person carrying a sunshade,' she began.

'It's an umbrella,' corrected Charlotte, peering over Miss Gaunt's shoulder.

'Of course – an umbrella – how silly of me. And waves – lots of waves.' She turned the cup about. 'Now I wonder what that can be?'

'A ship – it's a ship!' cried Charlotte. 'A ship with sails, as plain as plain!'

'And a tall gentleman wearing a top hat. Now who could that possibly be?'

'Papa,' said Charlotte promptly. 'I expect he'll bring me a present.' She lapsed into momentary silence, then sighed. 'I do wish he would stay away forever.'

*

The *Esmeralda* made fast alongside her berth in Brunswick dock, and James decided to stretch his legs by walking to the office.

There was a blustery, rain-laden wind blowing from the south-west, making James duck his head against sudden squalls gusting along the dock road. He wore seaman's garb of pea-jacket, check shirt worn, sailor-fashion, over a heavy woollen guernsey, and wide canvas trousers. Only his top hat distinguished him from any one of the seamen who populated the dock area. Settling his sea-bag more firmly upon his shoulder he threaded his way between twin rivers of traffic flowing to and from the docks, strode past cheap lodging houses, dance halls, noisy taverns and gin palaces, skirted a cluster of raddle-faced prostitutes, turned a corner and found himself facing Robert's departmental store. The transformation never ceased to surprise James. The old, once-familiar chandler's shop had metamorphosed, as though from a long-dormant pupa, through the chrysalis stage of grocer, to emerge in all its glory as the imago of the perfect merchant. It was an imposing building of stucco façade with windows of patent glass. Over the main entrance a pediment after the Greek style was supported by a pair of columnar figures representing a mermaid and a merman. A line of carriages waited outside and the shop seemed to be as busy as a bee-hive in spite of the raw wind which plucked at the ladies' skirts and funnelled a dancing trail of straw and paper along the street.

The shop now fronted almost the length of the street, its progress being halted by James's private entrance to his offices above and, like a down-at-heel neighbour leaning for support against a more affluent crony, a shabby block of nondescript offices with dusty windows, bearing in broken enamelled lettering the legend, *alt L ne & Co*.

James trotted up the two flights of stairs and pushed open the door of his outer office. The rows of clerks lifted their heads at his entrance, then with one accord bent over their work to scribble more industriously than ever. Mr Tupman, James's Chief Clerk, left his raised desk and hurried forward to greet his employer.

'A word in private with you, if you please, sir,' he said at the end of the civilities. Tucking his ledgers beneath one arm he followed James through to the private office. James dumped his sea-bag in one corner, settled into his desk chair selected a cigar and, as a mark of favour, offered the box to the waxen-faced clerk.

'Thank you, sir. I shall enjoy it later, if I may?' Protocol observed, Tupman placed the cigar in his pocket and stood waiting patiently, as expressionless as ever.

James struck a match, drew in a satisfying lungful of smoke, and surveyed Tupman through the wreathing, scented clouds. The man seemed to have aged but little since the day that Anne had discovered him, a trembling, drink-sodden wretch, half-starved, unemployed and unemployable, rescued him from the abyss of poverty and persuaded James to take him on at a wage of twelve shillings and six-pence a week. Tupman had taken the pledge and never looked back. His compendious knowledge of the world of shipping had raised him from humble scribbler to Chief Clerk and book-keeper at an honorarium of three hundred and fifty pounds. James, always prepared to recognise and reward merit, had added an annual bonus, considering it money well spent. Tupman was trustworthy, as efficient as a machine and, above all, activated by undeviating loyalty.

'Well, Mr Tupman,' he said at length. 'What seems to be the problem?'

'We are being raided,' said Tupman, and opened his ledgers.

'Raided?'

'Bulled,' said Tupman.

James shrugged. Members of the Stock Exchange often engaged in the game of bulls and bears. The bull would buy large blocks of shares, thereby artificially inflating the price, then sell at a profit. It was of little consequence to the company involved. The shares would change hands once or twice and then steady at their normal level.

'All our subsidiaries are affected.' Tupman shook his head. 'I don't understand it. Whoever is behind this is holding, not selling.'

44

James frowned. 'He's buying in?'

'It looks like it, sir.'

'Odd,' said James. 'Very odd. The man must have money to burn.' He drew thoughtfully upon his cigar. It didn't seem to make sense. He had founded the subsidiary companies with great skill, always ensuring that Onedin Line Limited remained the holding company with the lion's share of stock. No group of individuals could combine to seize control of even the smallest company. He ran his eye down the share register.

'His name does not appear, sir,' said Tupman. 'He's been buying through nominees.'

'He seems to have gone to an uncommon amount of trouble to conceal his identity,' grumbled James. 'And to little point, for he must be aware that I can smoke him out simply by calling a shareholders' meeting.'

'He may not attend,' conjectured Tupman.

'The man may be an eccentric,' replied James testily, 'but I doubt he's a fool.' He ran a finger down the column of figures. 'This venture must have cost him a mint.'

'Half a million. I have the figures here, sir.'

'Half a million!' James whistled. 'What the devil does the fellow hope to gain?'

James arrived home somewhat out-of-humour, to find Elizabeth taking tea with Charlotte and the starch-faced governess. .

The child looked up, round-eyed, slid from her chair and stood before him, wriggling shyly like an eel. He picked her up, gave her a self-conscious hug, hoisted her playfully towards the ceiling, then, lowering her to the floor, stood for a few moments looking down at the diminutive squirming figure, while he tried to articulate some form of affectionate parental greeting. The gulf was too wide, one that he had never been able to cross, so he resorted to clearing his throat and jerking open the fastenings of his sea-bag.

'If you rummage in there, you might find something to your liking, young lady,' he told her and turned to greet the others.

'Good afternoon, Miss Gaunt.' He noticed a purse of disapproval gathered about the governess's lips, and wondered what could have soured her stomach so quickly. They seemed to have been chattering like magpies when he entered the room.

She smiled politely. 'Good afternoon, Mr Onedin. I trust you made a successful voyage?'

'Successful enough,' he answered briefly, and gave his attention to Elizabeth's chatter.

There is not an ounce of affection in the man, Miss Gaunt thought. Small wonder the child was ill at ease in his presence. She watched Charlotte tumbling out the contents of the sea-bag and greedily ripping open the parcels. Two foreign-looking dolls, a comb and a mantilla of black lace had already come to light. She went to help the child to crow over the treasure trove.

'You must remember to thank your Papa,' she whispered, and stole a sidelong glance towards her employer. He was standing tall and straight, and a smile suddenly illuminated his features as though lit by an inner fire. A charmless man, she decided. One who could only reflect the warmth of others. She raised her eyes, met a disapproving stare from the portrait, and returned her attention to Charlotte who was tearing the wrappings from yet another package.

James, listening inattentively to Elizabeth's prattle, was gazing idly into a mirror over her shoulder. He caught a glimpse of the governess's inquisitorial glance, watched the tilt of her head as she turned back to Charlotte. Her lips curved into an ever-widening smile that was like opening a secret door. She was, he reflected, a woman singularly lacking in charm but, nevertheless, one well-suited to her situation. Something about her laughter, mingled with Charlotte's, plucked at a chord of memory. His eyes met the reflected image of Anne's benign gaze. There was, he thought, a certain facile resemblance. Not so much in the features, although both were, in all conscience, Plain Janes. It was something elusive about the creature's character . . .

'James!' Elizabeth interrupted his train of thought. 'You are not listening!' she accused.

46

'I am trying to listen,' he said irritably. 'But you do babble on so. You were saying that William has left the *Conway*.'

'That was hours ago!' wailed Elizabeth. 'Do pay attention. This is important.'

James sighed. Everything from a new bonnet to a plague of cockroaches was important to Elizabeth.

Elizabeth lowered her voice and composed her features into a suitably disconsolate frame. 'Poor Mr Frazer, but a shadow of his former self. It quite breaks my heart to see him so low. He has taken to his bed and is quite resigned to his end.'

'Death and taxes,' said James. 'There is no evading either.'

'He has expressed the wish that William carry on the good name of the business.'

'Laudable,' commented James drily. 'But hardly practicable under the circumstances.'

'William and his grandfather had a long, long, private conversation, after which the dear man made a new will. In it he bequeaths everything to William.'

'William won't inherit so much as a hank of rope yarn until he is of age,' James reminded her. 'In the meantime, who is to manage his affairs?'

'I am,' said Elizabeth determinedly.

James eyed her askance. 'You are? Really, Elizabeth, sometimes I think you live in cloud-cuckoo land. Have you the remotest idea what the management of a shipping company entails?'

'I should,' she replied tartly. 'I have been closely involved in the day-to-day administration of Frazer Line for the past two years.'

'Office work is one thing,' said James. 'Any competent clerk can handle it. But total responsibility is a different kettle of fish. Take my advice: when the time comes, sell out and invest the capital for William's coming of age. Otherwise you will be fleeced white.'

'I won't!' Elizabeth's jaw set into obstinate lines. 'I have given my word – the company will be handed over to William intact.'

James tried again. 'You will be dealing with rapacious

merchants who won't take kindly to dealing with petticoats.'

'So much the worse for them, for they will deal with me, or none at all.' She grinned and tossed back her mane of hair. 'I shall have them buzzing around me like bees around a honeypot.'

'No woman has ever appeared on the floor of the Exchange,' said James.

Her grin widened. 'Then it will be a new experience for the members.'

James sighed. All the Onedins could be mulishly obstinate when occasion required. Even Robert could be as immovable as a rock, once resolved upon a course of action.

'Think on it, Elizabeth, there is not only a fleet of ships to be kept afloat, crews to be paid, stores to be ordered, manifests, bills of lading ... '

'I have a most responsible Chief Clerk in Dunwoody. I shall rely upon him. As you rely upon your Tupman.'

'But,' pursued James, 'there are also the shipyards to consider — '

'Grist to the mill,' said Elizabeth. 'I can carry out repairs to my own ships at less than cost. And take a leaf from your book, James, and offset one company against the other.'

James shook his head. 'It won't work. Grant me that I know more of ships and ship construction than you, and let me assure you that I would not consider building so much as a rowboat unaided.'

'The world is changing,' said Elizabeth. 'Even Grandfather Frazer recognises that the days have long gone when one man gave his personal attention to the placing of every nut and bolt. Today we hire designers and engineers to carry out the buyer's specifications. All that is required is a measure of common sense and a sharp eye to costs.'

'You make it sound all so easy,' said James. He shrugged. 'Be it on your own head.'

Elizabeth shivered suddenly and wrapped her arms about herself. 'Someone is walking over my grave,' she said with mock humour. She stood beneath the portrait and warmed her hands at the fire.

'I am being followed,' she announced to the flickering tongues of flame guttering up the chimney.

James frowned. 'Followed? By whom?'

She turned to face him. 'I don't know. But wherever I go, whenever I turn my head, something – it – is there. A shadow, slipping away.'

'A what – ?'

The room lay still and quiet, while the rain tapped feverishly against the window-panes like the scrabblings of a dead man's fingers.

'A ghost,' said Elizabeth.

Chapter Four

There were ghosts everywhere. They flitted about the house like bats. Hanging from the ceilings, chattering in the shadows, howling in the throat of the wind.

Emma lay abed, her eyes running around the room like frightened mice. A ghost face loomed out of the darkness and a ghost voice droned: 'Being of sound mind and body...'

She was floating in a sea of fire and yet her veins ran with ice. If she closed her eyes she could see inside her skull. The ghost voice rang and echoed like a sonorous deep-toned bell. She opened her eyes again and peered out through heavily-shuttered lids.

A watery sun slanted through the lace curtains and set golden devil-motes dancing in the air. Shadows moved and drifted and she recognised Doctor Pritchard's features swaying above like an ungainly flower on a stalk. The other with the round moon-face and liturgical voice must be lawyer Goodwin. She looked beyond him to the open door, and beyond the door to a marble palace with strutting peacocks and silver trees with golden pomegranates. A charcoal brazier glowed and an almond-eyed amah held out a silver pipe.

'I don't like it,' said Pritchard. 'She is non compos mentis.'

'She was lucid enough when she gave her instructions,' replied the lawyer tartly. 'That is all that matters.'

She overheard, but the voices seemed to come from another world as she watched the palace filling with people.

There was her father, short and tubby, his bulldog features twisted into a grin of greeting. Her brother with his pale, drowned face not a day older. Her mother holding out imploring arms. And Daniel. Daniel Fogarty. *Do you take this woman to be your lawful wedded wife?* demanded the parson. *I do*, said Daniel and stepped into the room. 'How is she?' he asked.

'Failing,' said Pritchard. 'Failing fast.'

The door closed slowly, shutting off the palace with all its delights and imprisoning her in the room with its menacing shadows.

'Poor Emma,' said Daniel.

She shrank back into the pillows, burrowed her body beneath the bedclothes as his face ran like wax and rivulets of tears burned like acid.

'Poor Emma,' he said again. 'I treated you hardly. Forgive me, Emma.'

'Sign,' said Goodwin. 'Sign here, Mrs Fogarty. Just your signature.' He propped her up and pushed a pen between her fingers.

She stared at the blurred characters but obediently scrawled her signature. It was the least she could do for Daniel, she thought. Now he would know she loved him. Had always loved him. She looked up at the troubled face looming above her.

'Build temples,' she said. 'Many temples.'

'I shall,' he promised.

A kaleidoscope of memories flickered like old lantern slides. *China. The bridge across the Min river. Foochow. Doctor McRae with his wise old face, whisky breath, and dun-coloured bottles of cure-alls. The roar of guns, pirates swarming over the shipside, the half-naked body of the man she had killed as he burst into her room. The long race home, and Daniel's fury at being cheated of his prize. Anne. Anne who had been with child and suffered the torments of the damned as the ships smashed their way through the seas. The terror of loneliness, with the house echoing to her calls after Daniel fled across the world, taking that damned Delilah with him. The haunted days and the haunted nights with only the solace of the silver pipe for comfort.*

Incense floated into the room and its soft fumes filled her pumpkin head. The door opened again and the marble palace filled with light and the sound of tinkling silver bells. Anne stood framed in the doorway, smiling and beckoning.

She rose from her bed and swam forward, through the doorway and into the blinding light beyond. Then the door closed behind her and she fell headlong into darkness.

Doctor Pritchard lowered Emma's hand, reached forward and closed her eyes.

'She's gone,' he said.

The funeral took place on Wednesday morning, and Emma was laid to rest alongside her parents with a wild wind raging across a lowering sky and bringing flurries of snow to whiten the fresh-turned earth.

The mourners stood in a semicircle, wretched and cold, the numbing wind pinching their features blue and red as the Reverend Mr Magnus fluted his way through the service.

'Ershes to ershes, dast to dast,' he piped, as each took a turn at the trowel and cast a handful of red earth upon the brass-bound coffin below.

Emma had lived alone and died alone. Only the family attended the last rites. A few dead leaves scurried about their feet and Mr Magnus's thick melton cloak flapped and billowed about his white surplice as he gabbled his way towards the end of the ritual.

' . . . the fellowship of the Holy Ghost be with us all evermore amen,' he finished and hurriedly led his flock back to the waiting carriages.

Sarah, hunched beneath a long astrakhan coat, clutched Robert's arm for support and darted a glance towards Elizabeth. 'I don't know how she has the face to attend,' she proclaimed in a sibilant whisper. 'I mean, after all that – business – with you-know-who, you would imagine she would die of shame before setting foot on sacred ground!'

Robert flinched, well aware that one of Sarah's confidential whispers could penetrate an oaken door. 'For heaven's sake, Sarah,' he grumbled. 'Hold your tongue. All that is over and forgotten. Let the poor creature rest in peace.'

Sarah disengaged her arm. 'I'll just run across and offer a word of comfort. Elizabeth was never one for betraying her feelings, but I am sure she feels the situation most keenly.'

Robert watched her go, head down against the wind, face eager for snippets of gossip. He heard shreds of Sarah's voice, tossed by the wind. 'My dear Elizabeth. Such a bitter day for you . . . ' Then James sauntered by, head bowed in thought. Robert fell into step beside him and eyed the outlines of Miss Gaunt and Charlotte walking ahead.

'Handsome figure of a woman,' he offered.

James emerged from his brown study. 'What?'

'Your governess. Trim figure. Very trim. And can't have reached thirty yet, I'll be bound. I warrant she's no more than twenty-eight – twenty-nine at the outside.' He cocked his head knowingly and nudged his brother in the ribs. 'You certainly know how to pick 'em, you sly dog.'

James scowled at Robert's elephantine jocularity, conceded that Miss Gaunt was at all times of neat and tidy appearance, added that, in his eyes, her sole attributes lay in her ability to carry out her duties, and abruptly changed the subject.

'I have a project in mind which might prove of interest to you, Robert.'

Robert eyed him suspiciously. 'Oh?'

'You are an astute fellow,' said James. 'And I should like your opinion.'

Robert's suspicions deepened. When James handed out compliments it behoved a prudent man to take care.

'And what is this opinion to cost me?' he demanded.

'Not a penny piece,' said James smoothly. 'Unless, of course, you are of a mind to line your pockets.'

'Line them with promises, you mean.' Robert shook his head. 'No, James. Opinions cost nothing, but I have burned my fingers too often on the hob of your ambitions. In any event this is no place to discuss business.'

'I agree,' said James. 'Shall we say lunch? Tomorrow?'

'Very well,' agreed Robert, determining to indulge himself at James's expense. 'Where do you suggest?'

'At your club. I believe they do an excellent saddle of mutton.'

'My club!' expostulated Robert, realising that he would be expected to foot the bill. 'What is the matter with yours?'

'Too many shipping interests with sharp ears. Besides, yours is far more comfortable. And discreet.'

The mourners wound their way towards their carriages like so many black snails trailing through the gathering snow. A red sun peered balefully down like a probing, Cyclopean eye. The trees waved white shrouded arms and moaned and muttered among themselves.

Elizabeth paused at her carriage, looked back over her shoulder, and found the hair rising on the nape of her neck as a dark shadow moved between the gravestones. It seemed to be staring directly towards her. Its eyes glowed, reflecting the glare of the sun; then it was gone, swallowed in swirling clouds of snow.

As the carriage wended its way back home, wheels crunching, the horse's hooves kicking up clods of slush, she continued to shiver and tremble while her heart fluttered like an imprisoned bird. *He has come back*, she thought. *Back from the dead!*

'I never gave Albert a fair crack of the whip,' said Frazer, 'and it's a bit late in the day to make amends now, but I'm doing the best I can.'

He lay in the great four-poster bed, a shrunken simulacrum of his former self, arms as thin as sticks, face sunken and pinched into unnatural hollows. He switched his gaze from Elizabeth to William. 'Inheritance, that's the key. One day, young man, you will have childer of your own and come to understand the importance of progeniture. A tree must have strong roots, otherwise it will fall at the first gale. D'ye follow me, boy?'

'Uncle James does well enough,' said William.

The old man sighed, his breath whistling in his throat. 'A weak girl-child. It must be a bitter sorrow to him.'

'Don't overtax your strength,' warned Elizabeth.

'Death comes easily to the old,' said Frazer. 'It is the

young who struggle and fight. He has a right friendly face, has Death; and when he knocks at your door he comes as a welcome guest. Don't grieve for me when I'm gone, but lay me beside George Callon. There was a man – us'd been friends all us lives – we didn't always see eye to eye, and many a harsh word passed between us, but we had a deal of respect for each other.'

A fit of coughing shook his frame and a grimace of pain contorted his features. Elizabeth hurried towards the array of medicine bottles on his bedside table, but he waved her away. 'I've had enough of patent nostrums, I'll go to my end in peace, thank you.' He wheezed deep in his chest until he regained his breath. 'Poor Emma. The sins of the father shall be visited upon the children. That's Scripture and gospel true. George Callon made his money from the traffic, and his daughter – poor demented creature – died of it.' He grimaced at Elizabeth. 'You only knew him when he was old and set in his ways, but he were a hot-brained young fire-eater in his youth. Made his fortune in the opium trade.'

'Poor Emma,' said Elizabeth. 'All alone in that great, empty house.'

The old man nodded. 'Wi' naught but her dreams for company ever since that rascal Fogarty abandoned her.'

Elizabeth flushed at the mention of her past escapades as Frazer returned his attention to William.

'And how are you taking to office work, young man?'

'Very much so, thank you, Grandfather,' said William.

'He takes to it like a duck to water,' said Elizabeth. 'You were right, Grandfather, seafaring would have been no life for William.'

'And you?' pursued Frazer. 'Have you the confidence to hold the reins after I'm gone?'

Elizabeth leaned forward and deposited a kiss upon his forehead. 'You are an old rogue, you know perfectly well that I have been handling your affairs for the past six months. As a matter of fact, I have acquired quite a taste for it.'

'It's power,' said Frazer. 'Once bitten, there's no letting go.' The breath rasped in his chest and he sought her hand for comfort. 'Marry again,' he urged. 'Marry before it's too late. Business can be a demanding taskmaster. It is the worse for those that have a flair for it. Remember, William will take over one day, and when that day comes, you'll find yourself with no resources to fall back on. You don't want to end your days locked in dreams, like Emma.'

'I have no taste for opium,' said Elizabeth lightly.

'You'll need an opiate of one sort or another,' said the old man sagely. 'And I can think of none better than a houseful of childer and a husband. They would keep you occupied for the rest of your days.'

'Wasted days,' said Elizabeth. 'For I have little liking for domesticity.'

He wagged his head negatively upon the pillow. 'You are making a mistake. Get yourself wedded and bedded without delay. That's my advice, take it, or leave it.'

'I can take care of myself,' she said, settling the covers about him. 'Now it is time for your nap. Off to sleep with you.'

They left him, a crumpled figure with a rakish nightcap tilted over one eye, already breathing stertorously as he slid into the mists of his private dreams, and made their way downstairs. Jenny, the parlourmaid, had been waiting in the hallway. She rose from a chair, smoothed her skirts and bobbed a curtsy.

'Beg pardon, ma'am, but there's a genneman caller awaiting in the drawing room.'

Elizabeth frowned. 'A gentleman? To see me?'

'Wouldn't give no name, ma'am. Said it would be all right, you and him being well-acquainted.'

Elizabeth puzzled over the information. It seemed strange behaviour for someone claiming acquaintanceship not to present his card before making himself free of her drawing room.

'Seems a very well-to-do genneman,' volunteered Jenny. 'Dresses very fashionable. A clean-shaven genneman, as tall as a tree. Give me a half guinea for me trouble.'

'Very well, Jenny,' said Elizabeth. 'You may show me in.'

She and William entered the drawing room. She heard the loud snick of the closing door and the steady *tick-tock* of the long-case clock standing in the corner. The room seemed unnaturally still. The wind gusted against the snow-encrusted window panes, and the swagged velvet curtains billowed slightly as a tall figure emerged from the shadows to step forward to meet her.

His footfall was soft upon the carpet. She swayed and would have fallen had she not reached to William's shoulder for support. Her heart beat frantically and her mouth ran dry.

She found her voice at last. '*Daniel* . . . ? Is it you?'

She would have known him anywhere, in whatever guise. There was a touch of grey to his hair, and in place of the familiar beard he now sported a trim military moustache. His face was deeply tanned from long exposure to distant suns, and laughter-lines wrinkled the corners of his eyes. He wore an expensively cut, pearl-grey suit with a pearl-grey tie held in place by a gold stick-pin mounted with the largest pearl she had even seen. There was also a new-found confidence in his bearing, a spring to his step she had never known before, and he carried himself straight with the air of a man sure and certain of his authority.

He had changed, and yet he was still the same Daniel Fogarty she had known all those years ago. He had the same brown monkey-eyes with their slightly puzzled air, the same heavy jaw and white teeth, ever ready to break into a smile. She wanted to reach out and touch him, to stroke the beardless chin.

'Hullo, Elizabeth,' he said. His eyes belied the banality of his greeting, seeming to drink her in as though thirsting for the longed-for reality of her presence.

'Daniel – is it you? Really you?' The words came out in a whisper of disbelief.

He dragged away his gaze and eyed William quizzically. 'Aren't you going to introduce me?'

She began to gather her wits, remember the frail old man lying upstairs, nearing his end, dying in ignorance.

'This is my son, William,' she said, with the barest inflection of warning. 'William – this is your Uncle Daniel.'

'How do you do, sir?' said William politely.

The pair shook hands, then Daniel, arms akimbo, stood back a pace and surveyed William as though inspecting bloodstock at a fair.

He winked at Elizabeth. 'A chip off the old block, eh, Elizabeth? From the set of his shoulders I would say that he takes after his father.'

'People have remarked upon the resemblance,' said Elizabeth ambiguously.

Daniel grinned down at the boy. 'Well, young feller-me-lad, do you remember me?'

William puckered his brows in thought. 'Vaguely, sir, I recollect that I did once own acquaintance with an uncle Daniel. I believe he went abroad . . . ?'

'That's right, son. Off to make my fortune in Australia. I have made it – and now I'm back to claim my own.'

Elizabeth's heart missed a beat. She gave Daniel a warning glance and summoned up a smile. 'Be off with you, William, your Uncle Daniel and I have much to talk about.'

'Yes, Mama.' He paused before taking his leave and looked hesitantly at Daniel. 'I believe, sir, that you once wore a beard?'

Daniel laughed delightedly. 'That's right, my boy. A full round set of whiskers. Isn't that so, Elizabeth?'

She blushed at the memory and murmured an indistinct answer.

'Mama has an old photograph in a heavy silver mount upon her dressing table. It bears quite a distinct resemblance. You, sir, are holding an old-fashioned stove-pipe hat and standing stiff and straight beside Mama. It must have been taken a long time ago,' William added thoughtfully.

'It was,' said Daniel. 'Before you were born, but I recollect the occasion as though it were yesterday. Don't you, Elizabeth?'

She returned his secret smile. 'But of course. I am reminded every day.'

Daniel put a fatherly hand on William's shoulder and gently propelled him towards the door. 'Off with you, my boy. Your mother and I have business to discuss.'

William paused at the door. 'I trust I may have the pleasure of renewing our acquaintance in the near future,' he said with formal politeness.

'You can bet your boots on it, cobber,' said Daniel.

'Cobber?' William looked puzzled. 'Yes, sir,' he said, and closed the door behind him.

Daniel reached out and held Elizabeth at arm's length while his gaze searched her face. 'Not a day older,' he breathed. 'I'll take my oath on it.'

Elizabeth disengaged herself, pushed aside a stray wisp of hair, and smiled uncertainly. 'I owe time a mounting debt, which some day, no doubt, I shall be required to pay. The years have not been unkind to you, either, Daniel.'

'Hard living,' said Daniel lightly. 'It tones the muscles.' He eyed her dress approvingly. 'The fashion becomes you.'

'A vast improvement on the crinoline,' she said, laughing. 'All those hoops and whalebone. So constricting.'

'I remember,' said Daniel.

They stood smiling at each other, looking back into the past, old memories rekindled. He took a tentative step forward and the blood pounded in her head, became a monstrous tidal surge.

'Dear Daniel,' she said over and over again. 'Dear, dear Daniel . . .'

At length she twisted free and stood breathless and swaying with a witless dizziness that turned her bones to rubber and her brain into a phantasmagoria of tormenting images.

Daniel inflated his cheeks and expelled a long-held breath. 'That settles it,' he proclaimed. 'We shall marry as soon as may be.'

She wanted to respond, 'Oh, yes, Daniel, oh, yes, yes, immediately,' but the memory of Grandfather Frazer put a bridle on her tongue. He was a hard, unforgiving man, with a malevolent hatred for Daniel Fogarty that knew no bounds, blaming him for the death of his son. Even a whisper that Daniel had so much as entered the house would be enough to send him into a fit of ungovernable rage; and the merest hint of William's true paternity would result at the very least in the loss of William's promised patrimony, and the probability that both would be bundled out of house and home.

True, Daniel would support them, but there was a vast difference between a life of luxury and as wife to a ship's captain . . .

She shook her head violently. 'No, wait – wait, Daniel. I must have time to think.'

'Goose,' he said. 'What is there to think about?'

'William,' she began desperately. 'He must never know.'

His manner hardened a little. 'Of course he must know. He *is* my son.' He tried to assuage her fears. 'We shall break it to him gently. Not immediately, but in the course of time. I shall play the part of Uncle Daniel for a week or two, gain his confidence . . .'

A week or two. She stared at him, horrified. 'The scandal,' she said, clutching at straws. 'Think of the scandal.'

He pooh-poohed her objections. 'A nine days' wonder, soon to be forgotten.' He flicked at an imaginary speck of dust upon the sleeve of his tailored jacket and spoke with the assurance of a man confident of his authority. 'We shall take our place in society. Believe me, there will be few who will have the temerity to cross me.'

Elizabeth stared at him. This was a different Daniel. No longer the mawkish, tongue-tied young man, forever cawing in his throat, whom she had loved, so long ago. This Daniel was a horse of a different colour: self-contained, with even a hint of arrogance in his bearing. She doubted she would be able to twist this version around her little finger as easily as she had the old.

He thrust his hands deep into his pockets and stood straddle-legged before her. 'I am no penniless wanderer, Elizabeth. Were Albert alive today I could match him a gold piece for every penny he could muster.'

She smiled at his naïvety. 'I trust that you are not suggesting that I was ever for sale to the highest bidder.'

'Of course not,' he assured her gravely. 'But if you were, even I could not afford you.'

'Well, well,' she laughed, 'it would seem that your absence in the colonies has not only made you rich, but taught you gallantry into the bargain.'

'It taught me more than that.' He moved across to the

60

fireplace and stood with his back to the fire as though taking possession of the room and waited broodingly as she settled herself attentively in an armchair of ruby velvet trimmed with braids of red and gold silk.

The house creaked and sighed, groaned with the weight of age and the passage of years as he spoke of his early days, of his successes and failures, of his one-time partner . . .

'Tom Macauley. His folks were transported felons, back around 1820, that would be. When Tom came of age he was given a grant of land – it's the custom Down-under – Currency lads, they called them. When I first met him he had land, but no stock. I had capital but no experience. We put the two together and in a few years we had a station the size of Wales and more sheep than we could count . . .'

She listened enthralled to his accounts of drought and pestilence; of fights with black men painted in the likeness of devils; of bush-rangers; of kangaroos and wallabies. He used words and phrases totally unfamiliar to her ears, and as he unconsciously slipped back into the speech cadences of his adopted country, the twanging Australian drawl became more and more pronounced. *He has changed*, she thought. *More than I would have believed possible.*

' . . . and then we struck gold,' he was saying.

'A gold mine?'

He grinned at the note of incredulity in her voice. 'I thought that would impress you. We split the profits fifty-fifty, then one day I took stock, counted my blessings and sold out my end.' His grin broadened. 'So here I am, as large as life, and ready to show some of your local silvertails a thing or two.'

She gnawed at her lower lip as she tried to wrestle with the problem of an affluent Daniel Fogarty suddenly erupting into her life. He certainly looked the part of a man who had made the world his oyster, but appearances could be deceptive, and no doubt a small fortune went a long way in a far-off colony peopled by outcasts and painted savages; but in a country where millionaires rubbed shoulders in the street that same fortune could soon be made to look like small change. She remembered the story of Lionel Melchior in *The Prodigal's Return,* in which the long absent Lionel returned determined to cut a figure in society, only to end his days in a debtors' prison.

'I have a few old scores to settle,' he said, and banged a fist into the palm of his hand. 'There are one or two who will be jumping to a different tune when I whistle, I promise you.'

She grimaced. 'Don't be a fool, Daniel. Old scores are like old sores, picking at them only makes them worse. Moreover, much has happened since you have been away. James has fingers in many pies and ... '

'I know,' said Daniel. 'I know all there is to know about James's activities. And yours, my dear.'

'Mine?'

'Oh, I have been keeping an eye on you. From a safe distance.' He smiled like a benign uncle.

'So it was you who have been following me?' She shook her head. 'I don't understand?'

He shrugged. 'I had to be certain.'

'Of what?'

'Of you. Confound it,' he added with a touch of exasperation, 'it should be plain enough. You might very well have remarried and had a brood of children for ought I knew.'

'Dear Daniel,' she said softly. 'There could never be anyone else.'

He took a step towards her and drew her to her feet. She slipped into his arms, yearning to return to those yesterdays so long ago.

'Daniel,' she murmured. 'Dear, dear Daniel.'

'There, there,' he said. 'My dearest, dearest love.'

Her veins flamed with fire, tears scalded her eyes and she shook and shivered as though with the ague. But while he muttered and murmured imbecilities part of her brain gnawed at the problem of William and his inheritance. Needing time to think before her treacherous body betrayed her irredeemably, she wriggled free and patted straying tendrils of hair back into place.

He, too, seemed to require a breathing space for he moved away to take up his former stance before the fire.

'Now that there are no further obstacles in the way,' he began.

She cut him short. 'Obstacles? Is that how you viewed Emma? As an obstacle in your path?'

'Poor Emma,' he said contritely. 'She deserved better than me.'

'You knew of her death?'

He nodded. 'I was at her bedside.'

She smoothed her dress. '*And* at the funeral. I think it time we had a long talk, Daniel.'

She told him how William now had one foot in the business, of Grandfather Frazer's will. 'Signed, sealed and witnessed,' she said. 'Nothing must be allowed to stand in William's way. Not even you, Daniel.'

'I have no intention of standing in the boy's way, Elizabeth. On the contrary, I am determined to help him in every way I can.'

'If Grandfather Frazer learns that you and I have so much as passed the time of day he will alter his will, so the best service you can render William is to quietly disappear into wherever you have been hiding yourself these past few weeks.'

'Months,' he corrected. He rubbed his chin thoughtfully. 'Vindictive as ever, is he?'

'He has never forgiven you, Daniel,' she told him, while her mind stored away this latest nugget of information. Daniel had been home for months, not weeks.

He laughed. 'Don't worry, my love. I can buy and sell a dozen Grandfather Frazers.'

She stared at him, uncomprehending.

'You don't understand, Elizabeth,' he said gently. 'I am a millionaire.'

'A millionaire? You – ?'

He nodded gravely. 'Several times over.'

Chapter Five

The hansom creaked and jolted over the cobbles. There came a sound like the tearing of sheets and a gale of evil-smelling wind filled the confines of the cab.

Robert clapped a handkerchief to his nose. 'My God!' he choked. 'What on earth have you been feeding the beast?'

The whiskered jarvey, perched high above his passenger's head, grinned through yellowed teeth, leaned forward and called hoarsely through the open roof trap. 'Mash 'n' 'ay. Keeps 'er in good pecker.'

The hansom drew to a halt at the kerbside. Robert thankfully pushed open the splash doors and clambered wheezily down to the pavement. He handed the man his fare and added a shilling tip. 'Buy the creature a bag of oats,' he commanded sourly and made his way to the wide portico of his club.

These days he was inclined to lean a little more heavily upon his stick and he found himself puffing from the exertion of mounting the short flight of steps. A liveried doorman in gold-braided top hat swept open the glass-fronted doors with a flourish and in the richly carpeted foyer a second flunkey took Robert's hat, coat and stick. Pausing before a tall mirror inset in the panelled wall Robert adjusted his tie, smoothed his hair and stood for a moment narcissistically eyeing his reflection. His frock coat fitted like a glove and although the buttons tended to strain against his stomach he had, he considered, the figure to carry it off. A touch of grey in hair and moustache lent an air of distinction to a face comfortably padded with good living and reflecting the image of a man of substance.

Satisfied with his appraisal he made his way to the smoking room, a paunchy figure with heavy jowls and face mapped with a network of tiny red veins, watery blue eyes pouched in layers of fat – a pompous man content with his place in the ordained order of things.

He found James already settled in an armchair by the window, his long legs stretched out before him and one of his favourite black cigars, with a growing cone of ash, clenched between his teeth.

'You are late,' he commented as Robert lowered himself into the chair opposite.

'Three minutes,' said Robert, scowling at his watch and irritated at being taken to task by his guest. 'Traffic,' he added grumpily. 'The streets are choked with traffic. It would be quicker to walk.'

'And more beneficial,' said James. 'You are putting on weight, Robert. You should take more exercise.'

'Unhealthy,' said Robert. 'Too much exercise deranges the functions of the body.'

He ordered a pre-luncheon stomach-crisper of brandy and soda and gazed owlishly at his brother. 'Well, James, what is this scheme upon which you so urgently require an opinion?'

James dipped down to the side of his chair, fished up a worn leather satchel and extracted a thin sheaf of papers bound with pink ribbon and enscribed in Mr Tupman's cursive script: *Prospectus. An Invitation to the Public.*

Robert turned over the page and his lips moved silently as though in prayer as he slowly digested the information. He paused, read and re-read a paragraph, then raised his head to stare aghast at James. 'Five – million ... ?'

'Pounds,' said James.

'Madness,' said Robert.

'There is plenty of spare money in the City,' said James.

'You will find no takers,' said Robert. He tapped the prospectus. 'Not on this evidence.'

'It is only a rough draft,' said James testily. 'Naturally, I

65

shall make one or two amendments before sending it to the printers.'

Robert snorted. 'You will need to. There will be few fish rising to this bait.'

'Then more fool they,' said James. 'For it is the chance of a lifetime.'

'A chance to land in Queer Street, more like.' Robert took a savouring taste of his brandy and soda and shook his head sagaciously. 'If ever a venture was doomed to failure from the start, this is it.'

James expelled a breath of exasperation. 'If ever there was a man blessed with the ability of sniffing out success and pronouncing it failure, that man is you, Robert.'

'You canvassed my opinion and I have given it,' said Robert stiffly.

James sniffed. 'One which is hardly worth the expense of a lunch. Be specific, man. What, in your view, are the drawbacks?'

Robert once more applied himself to the prospectus. 'As I understand it you are proposing to build a port, complete with harbour and rail facilities, in some outlandish place that no one has ever heard of. If this haven has such potential, why has it never been discovered before?'

'It is windbound,' said James.

Robert spread his hands. 'There you are then.'

'Steamships,' said James gently, 'have one great virtue. They pay little attention to head winds.'

'Steamships.' Robert blew through his moustache. 'For a man with heavy investments in sail you seem to be in an uncommon hurry to give the advantage to your competitors.'

'Whoever owns the port, controls the charges,' said James.

'You speak here of opening up the interior for trade. But as I understand it, this harbour is land-locked and separated from the hinterland by a swift-moving river at the bottom of a chasm.' Robert wrinkled his nose. 'Not the most enticing prospect for would-be investors.'

'A bridge, a railhead and a road. That is all that is

66

required.' James gazed out of the window. 'Look into the street, Robert, and tell me what you see.'

Robert stared and shrugged his shoulders. 'Nothing out of the ordinary. Passers-by. A horse and cart. A greengrocer. A butcher. A shoe-maker. A row of houses.'

'People,' said James, 'and all making a profit, the one from the other. What do they have in common? They have clothes to their backs and boots to their feet. They live in houses built mainly of timber. Timber joists and timber floor-boards. They drink coffee, eat meat, and there is hardly a sideboard without its bowl of fruit. There's the trade, Robert. Right on your doorstep.'

'We've been trading with Brazil for donkey's years,' said Robert. 'Those markets have long been spoken for.'

'The State of Parana,' James explained patiently, 'has forests of timber, vast herds of cattle, plantations of cotton, orchards of oranges, but only two outlets – Santos, far to the north, and Port Alegre to the south. I intend to build a port in between.'

'It has merit,' Robert acknowledged grudgingly. 'But there is a catch to it somewhere.'

'If there is,' said James. 'I have yet to find it. Shall we go to lunch?'

They lunched off a couple of guinea fowl apiece larded with bacon, stuffed with chestnuts and served to the accompaniment of bread sauce, roast potatoes and buttered Brussels sprouts. Robert ordered a bottle of claret, drank most of it himself and finished the meal with a piece of ripe Stilton and a glass of crusty port. He signed the bill with a magisterial flourish and burped into his napkin.

James cracked a walnut, prised out the kernel and chewed reflectively for a few moments.

'Business good?' he asked eventually, with the bored air of a man who cares not one whit for the answer.

'Couldn't be better,' declared Robert. 'People seem to have money to burn, these days. The shop is crowded to the door, and even with extra assistants we are at our wits' end to cope with the demand.'

'You should extend,' advised James. 'No successful business can afford to stand still.'

'I wish you would take your own advice and move to other premises,' Robert retorted. 'How the devil can I extend when you keep the entire upper floor for yourself?'

'I see little point in change for change's sake, and new offices are hideously expensive, apart from being put to the bother of moving.' James yawned. 'I am quite comfortable where I am, thank you, Robert.'

Robert gloomily contemplated the prospect of being saddled with James and his horde of scurrying clerks to the end of his days. It was, in his considered opinion, worse than an infestation of mice.

'If you can't move up, move sideways,' said James. 'What of those offices on the corner? They are dilapidated enough to tumble about the occupants' ears. You should be able to pick them up for a song.'

'I've had my eye on them for some time,' said Robert. 'But the owner is a slippery customer. A chap named Sinclair. He runs a company called Salt Line.'

'Salt Line?' James shook his head. 'I've never heard of it.'

'Oh, it exists,' said Robert. 'It is a small one-man affair with four or five ships. Topsail schooners and a couple of ketches. They trade with North Wales for slate. Bricks for the Isle of Man. That sort of thing. Although I gather their ships seem to spend more time in port than at sea and are in as ramshackle a condition as their offices.'

'A run-down, one-man company?' James mused thoughtfully. 'Why not make an offer for the lot, lock, stock and barrel? If the company is in danger of going to the wall, this Sinclair will probably be glad to get it off his hands.'

'Buy him out?' Robert shook his head firmly. 'I have no intention of paying through the nose for a tumbledown heap of bricks and mortar. I'll bide my time.'

'And let someone else snap it up from under your nose?'

'I have no wish to be saddled with a handful of useless ships,' retorted Robert peevishly.

'As to that, I might be able to help you,' said James casually. 'If they are of seaworthy condition, and the price is right, I might consider taking them off your hands.'

'At bargain rates, no doubt. No, James, it won't do. I shall make an offer for the building alone, and he can take it, or leave it.'

James shrugged. 'Suit yourself.' He cracked another walnut. 'Just what is so slippery about your Mr Sinclair?'

'He never seems to be in his office – and such offices as you have never seen. Dust and grime everywhere. A couple of seedy-looking clerks idling their time and managed by an ill-mannered old curmudgeon who made it abundantly clear that visitors were not welcome.' Robert wagged his head. 'I am almost persuaded that this fellow Sinclair does not exist.'

'If he does,' said James, 'then a letter should elicit a reply. Particularly if it is couched in the vaguest of terms with the promise of easy money as the bait.'

Robert nodded agreement. 'And if there is no reply?'

'That,' said James, 'I leave to your imagination.'

Robert wrote his letter that same afternoon, posted it in the box at the corner of the street, and stood for long moments staring at the sooty façade of the Salt Line offices. As usual they seemed to be as deserted as a haunted house. He was concentrating his imagination on visualising the changes he would make once he could lay his hands upon the property, when he thought he saw a pale grey face peering at him through one of the grimy upper-storey windows. He shivered and almost jumped out of his skin as a hand clapped him upon the back and a once-familiar voice boomed, 'Hullo, Robert. Day-dreaming again, I see.'

Robert turned and gaped at the tall, grinning stranger. Recognition came slowly. 'Daniel!' he exclaimed at last. 'Daniel Fogarty! By all that's holy, I hardly recognised you!' He pumped the apparition warmly by the hand.

'I have been admiring your shop,' said Daniel. 'You really have come up in the world, Robert.'

'I haven't done too badly,' Robert admitted modestly.

'A retail store, no less. A far cry from the oil shop, eh?'

'Actually it is a departmental shop but we thought the

description too clumsy, so decided upon retail.'

'We have nothing like it in Australia,' said Daniel admiringly. He cocked his head. 'But I see that James still retains possession of the upper deck.'

'He sticks like a limpet,' said Robert gloomily. 'There is no shifting him.'

'Too bad,' said Daniel sympathetically. 'The acquisition of a second floor could make a vast difference.'

'I know, I know,' groaned Robert. 'But James won't budge.'

'The same old James?'

'He hasn't changed,' said Robert expressively. 'Except for the worse.' He belched as a mixture of port and over-ripe Stilton made its presence known. 'Would you care to look over the premises?' he asked with the insouciant air of a man confident of his achievements.

'I should be more than delighted,' said Daniel, and followed Robert through the imposing portico with its doors of patent glass locked back to allow the free entry of the public and a cold February wind.

Shop-walkers in tail coats and high, stiff collars conducted them from one department to another while Robert, in his natural element, roamed from counter to counter, inviting his guest to finger this and admire the texture of that. Bales of linen were unrolled for Daniel's inspection, rolls of curtain material for his approval, cylinders of linoleum for his admiration.

The shop was thronged with customers. Page-boys in smart blue uniforms scurried about carrying the bulkier parcels to the waiting carriages outside. Ladies in fur-trimmed coats and fashionable bonnets swept majestically from one department to another, picking and choosing as they went. Other ladies of lesser quality combed the haberdashery and millinery departments for spools of bright-coloured ribbons, richly emblazoned shawls and festoons of Nottingham lace. The assistants bowed, nodded and smiled as they demonstrated their wares, scribbled bills and parcelled packages. The shop-walkers moved about with lofty airs and all-seeing eyes. Steam pipes crackled, heating the air to greenhouse temperature.

'We open at eight and close at seven, with a late night on Fridays and Saturdays,' Robert told a perspiring Daniel. 'Half-day closing on Wednesdays. The assistants have half an hour for lunch and live out.'

Daniel congratulated Robert on this evidence of business acumen and thankfully followed him to the seclusion of his private office.

Space being at a premium it was small, but by no means cramped, and furnished with an eye to comfort. A bow-fronted grate glowed peacefully between brass andirons and a polished coal scuttle. Wainscotting of quarter-sawn oak lined the walls and bobbed velvet curtains hung across the windows to shield the occupant from all but the most insistent of draughts.

While Robert dispensed whisky and water from his private stock Daniel loosened his top coat, settled into a brocaded armchair and, realising that he was expected to sing for his supper, embarked upon an account of his Australian adventures.

At the end of the story Robert blew out his cheeks. 'What a tale! Sheep and gold mines! It is past belief! Just wait until Elizabeth hears!'

'How is she?' asked Daniel, tongue in cheek.

'In fine fettle,' said Robert. He winked knowingly. 'I think she still has a soft spot for you, Daniel.'

'I have long looked forward to renewing our acquaintance,' said Daniel ambiguously.

'Ah,' said Robert. 'Now there, there might be a problem.'

'Oh?'

'Mr Frazer.'

'I understand,' said Daniel. 'It must be handled discreetly. I am sure that I can rely upon your good offices, Robert.'

Robert shuddered at the thought of being involved in one of Elizabeth's intrigues. On the other hand, Daniel was evidently a man of substance and, as such, one whose patronage could well be worth the soliciting.

'Naturally, I should be only too delighted to do all in my

power, but . . . ' he raised his eyes heavenwards, 'I am simply not my own master, these days. The demands of business take up every minute of my time.'

Daniel smiled sympathetically. 'I quite understand. What I had in mind was a small dinner party. Just family.'

'An excellent suggestion,' Robert agreed warmly. 'A quiet little gathering should break the ice nicely. And what is more, no tongues can wag.'

'My thoughts entirely,' said Daniel. 'The only problem is where to have it. I have, for the moment, taken up residence in furnished apartments which, although comfortable, offer little in the way of culinary achievements.'

'Say no more!' Robert exclaimed. 'You shall dine with us. No, not another word, I beg of you. We have a most excellent cook and Sarah will be overjoyed at the prospect.' He waved away Daniel's protestations. 'We shall kill the fatted calf, and perhaps preface the repast with a dozen oysters.' He smacked his lips at the prospect, reached for the decanter, insisted upon Daniel's accepting a further two fingers and poured a generous measure for himself.

Affluence had wrought few changes in Robert, Daniel reflected. True, he had cut his cloth to suit his figure, but he remained the same bovine, self-opinionated windbag, as easily manipulated as a puppet on a string, that he had always been.

'I trust that James will honour us with his presence?' he inquired politely.

'If he smells money in the offing wild horses would not keep him away,' said Robert. 'Take my advice and give him a wide berth. He has some madcap, get-rich scheme for opening up the interior of Brazil, at a cost – can you credit it? – of five million!'

Daniel whistled. 'Five million? A tidy sum. How does he propose to raise it?'

'By public subscription. Don't be tempted, Daniel, James is as sharp as a weasel. If you should be looking for investments you could do no better than Consols. Consols are always with us.'

Daniel smiled. 'I shall try to remember.'

72

Robert broke the news to an excited Sarah and took refuge from her gabbling tongue by pleading an indisposition of the stomach and taking himself off to an early bed, where he fell into an uneasy sleep, to be haunted by dreams of a ghastly-visaged Mr Sinclair rising from beneath the floor-boards whence his murdered body had been consigned by a coven of blood-bespattered demon clerks.

He awoke with a yell, to find sunlight filtering through the windows and Mabel, the grey-haired housemaid, rattling the cups and saucers on their early-morning tea tray.

He shaved and dressed quickly, then, head aching abominably, went downstairs to breakfast off a pair of kippers and open his morning mail, while Sarah continued to prattle on as though there had been no interlude.

'It could not have happened at a more opportune moment,' she was saying. 'It will be half-term at Samuel's school and we shall have the dear boy home for a few days. I must remember to send him a hamper, I am sure they do not feed him properly.'

'They should feed like fighting cocks on the money I pay,' grumbled Robert. He picked a kipper bone from between his teeth and opened another letter. 'Well, well, well,' he announced. 'Our mysterious Mr Sinclair has risen to the bait.' He glanced at the postmark. 'Doesn't let the grass grow under his feet. Requests the pleasure of my company at his club, the Cadogan, at eleven this morning.'

Sarah wrinkled her forehead. 'The Cadogan? Where is that?'

'I have no idea,' said Robert. 'But no doubt the cabby will know.'

The cab driver did and, promptly at eleven o'clock, Robert found himself outside a discreet-looking building with basket-work across the lower halves of the windows and a pair of glass doors protected by wrought-iron grilles twined into the shape of forget-me-nots.

A flunkey in powdered wig and velveteen breeches took his hat, coat and stick, and conducted him to a room which seemed to be all plush and gilt, with tall mirrors reflecting

73

pillars ornately carved with the representations of fauns and satyrs in pursuit of scantily-clad nymphs.

The footman ushered him to a table secluded behind a potted palm. A tall, lean man with silver hair came to his feet and offered a languid hand.

'Mr Onedin? Sinclair. Delighted to make your acquaintance, old chap. You will take a little something?'

Before Robert could reply Sinclair nodded to the attendant. 'Mr Onedin will take the same.' He flapped a hand towards the chair opposite. 'I trust you will accept my recommendation? Brandy and champagne. I find it wondrously settling. Activates the juices and promotes the appetites.'

Robert eased himself into the chair and smiled weakly at his new acquaintance. Sinclair had a young-old face marked, if Robert was any judge, by lines of dissipation. He affected a flower in the buttonhole of his morning suit which, although well pressed, showed signs of the threadbare wear associated with a limited wardrobe.

'Thank you. Most kind,' he said. 'Although I am happy to say that I have always been of good appetite.'

Sinclair raised an eyebrow. 'Really? Without the aid of stimulants? I envy you, Mr Onedin, I do indeed.' He pursed his lips and steepled his fingers. 'And now, sir, in what way may I be of service to you?'

'I understand, Mr Sinclair, that you own the property next to mine?' said Robert, taking the bull by the horns.

'Next to yours?' Sinclair stifled a yawn. 'Of course, you are the shopkeeping Onedin, not the – ah – other one? I am afraid I have not as yet availed myself of the pleasure of visiting your establishment. Pressures of business, you understand? Actually I am in residence with an aged aunt. Lives in Croxteth Road. No doubt, as a tradesman, you are familiar with the area?'

Robert choked back his temper. 'I live there myself.'

Sinclair turned an insolent gaze upon Robert. 'Really? One never knows who one's neighbours may be, these days.'

A waiter arrived with their drinks. Sinclair spilled a handful of coins upon the tray with the carelessness of a man to whom money is no object, savoured his drink and smiled benignly. 'You were saying?'

Robert determined to give as good as he got. He pushed his glass to one side untasted and subjected Sinclair to a frosty gaze. 'I take it that you do fully represent Salt Line interests?'

'My dear chap, I am Salt Line. Do you take snuff?'

'No,' said Robert.

'Very wise. An insidious habit.' Sinclair helped himself to a generous pinch from a silver snuff box. 'And now, if you would be kind enough to come to the point?'

'I am considering the possibility of expanding my premises, and the thought crossed my mind that you might be open to an offer,' said Robert.

'And what sort of offer do you have in mind, Mr Onedin?'

Robert rolled his eyes towards the ceiling as though seeking inspiration. 'Two hundred?'

He met a blank stare.

'And fifty?'

Sinclair yawned. 'My dear sir, such a sum would barely compensate me for the nuisance of moving to new premises.'

'I'll go to three hundred,' said Robert, 'and pay the expense of removal.'

Sinclair smiled blandly and shook his head.

Robert transferred his gaze from the ceiling to the frieze surmounting one of the pillars and depicting a nymph with a look of alarm upon her face evading the grasp of a goat-footed satyr. Glancing in the mirror opposite he saw the reflected image of the fate which lay in store for the young maiden. Hastily averting his eyes he returned his attention to Sinclair. The man was obviously playing a cat and mouse game for some dubious reason of his own.

'Let us not beat about the bush,' said Robert. 'I'll put up a thousand in gold. And not a penny more. Take it, or leave it.' He watched Sinclair closely and imagined he saw an air of desperation behind the mask of polite indifference.

Sinclair drained his glass. 'Drink up, Mr Onedin. No heel taps, if you please.'

'Thank you, no. In my view champagne is fit only for

women and weaklings,' said Robert insultingly and had the satisfaction of seeing two red spots of anger flushing Sinclair's cheeks. He clasped his hands across his stomach and leaned back. 'I have offered several times the value of the property, Mr Sinclair, so what exactly is the problem?'

'There is no problem, Mr Onedin, and if there were I should account it none of your business.' Sinclair snapped his fingers and the waiter hurried forward. 'You prefer stronger waters, I understand?'

'Not at this hour of the morning,' said Robert. He waited until the manservant had taken an order for a second champagne and brandy. 'Name your price,' he said, and watched to see which way the cat would jump.

'My dear sir,' said Sinclair irritably. 'Can you not get it into your head that I have not the slightest desire to sell?'

'Nor, apparently, the wish to keep your property in a fit state of repair,' countered Robert.

'I find that remark most offensive,' snapped Sinclair and half rose from the table.

'Fifteen hundred,' said Robert, dangling the carrot.

'Good day to you,' said Sinclair coldly. Beads of perspiration stood upon his brow and his hands trembled from the effort of keeping himself under control.

Robert took his leave and, crossing the room, caught sight of Sinclair's reflection as the man reached out for Robert's untasted drink and swallowed it at a gulp. Collecting his hat, coat and stick, he exchanged a guinea for a vein of information and then made his way thoughtfully to James's office.

'He seems an odd fish, a very odd fish,' said James after Robert had recapitulated the story of his morning's conversation.

'He is all of that,' agreed Robert. 'He gave me a very warm time until I took his measure. When I offered fifteen hundred I thought he would have a fit.'

'Fifteen hundred? For that heap of old brickwork?' James looked askance at his brother's owlish features. 'You must be mad.'

'Or he is,' said Robert. 'I had not the slightest intention of paying such a sum, I merely wanted to discover how far he was prepared to go.'

James pulled at his nose. 'A man of extravagant tastes, you say?'

'According to the doorman he spends money like water, plays the tables, and has a fondness for the ladies.'

'And he turned down fifteen hundred pounds for a building worth – what?'

'A couple of hundred or so,' said Robert.

James shrugged. 'Then he is either very wealthy, or a fool.'

Robert shook his head. 'I would mark him down as a spendthrift, but no one's fool.'

'You are quite sure that he does fully represent Salt Line?'

'That was his very expression,' said Robert firmly. ' "I am Salt Line," he said.'

James drummed thoughtfully upon the desk top. 'A curious situation and one that bears looking into. Perhaps I should sound out your Mr Sinclair?'

'I have no objection,' said Robert. 'Provided that you remember whose money you are spending. Not one penny more than three hundred, James.'

'I'll bear it in mind,' said James, and marked down the small fleet of ships for himself.

Chapter Six

Seas of cloud lapped lakes of blue sky. A fresh wind blew steadily from the north-west and sent banners of chimney smoke streaming across the river. A pot-bellied shunting engine monotonously clanged its bell as it wheezingly dragged a row of clanking trucks along the dock road. Lines of cart-horses nuzzled their feed bags as they stood nose to tailboard patiently awaiting their turn to move to the loading berths.

James made his way to Coburg Dock, skirted transit sheds overflowing with cargoes of coffee, sugar, fruit and dyewoods, and crossed the footbridge to South Basin. Here a huddle of ships clung together as though for mutual support. He glanced at the houseflags flapping at the gaffs and found the one he sought. It was a tattered blue flag bearing a white diamond, in the centre of which were the barely discernible letters S–L.

The ship was a ketch of about three hundred tons and showed every sign of neglect: ropes frayed, decks grimy, canvas ill-patched and threadbare, paint peeling, teakwork unvarnished. A scruffy-looking individual wearing a greasy out-at-elbows guernsey and a three-day growth of beard was sucking at a stub of clay pipe and leaning negligently against the rail.

James gave him a hail. 'Who is in command?'

The man slowly removed the pipe from his mouth and poked the stem at his chest. 'I am.'

James eyed him frostily. 'Where will I find the Owner?'

The man blew into the bowl of his pipe. 'At home. Lying abed.'

James stared. 'In bed? At this hour of the day?'

'Allus abed,' said the man. 'I mean, she's a cripple, poor soul.'

'She?' James looked puzzled. 'Who is she?'

The man jerked a thumb towards the faded houseflag. 'Mrs Salt. The Owner. That's who you're looking for, i'n't it?'

'Mrs Salt,' said James, enlightened. He took a half crown from his pocket and flipped it into the air. 'Would you happen to know her address?'

She lived in a gaunt house buried amid a tangle of shrubbery. Her bedroom was an invalid's room. A room of muted colours with a pale wash of yellow sunlight filtering through curtained windows. It was a room choked with memories. Varnished oil paintings of gothic castles, of ships in storm and wrack, hung on the walls: a portrait of a stern-looking, bewhiskered Captain Salt, staring into eternity, took pride of place. Stuffed birds and animals, wax fruit and timeless clocks, were sheltered beneath glass domes. The furniture was heavy and monumental, crowding around a large half-tester bed shrouded with the swooping folds of lace curtains.

An old lady with a nut-cracker face wrenched by suffering, her hunched back propped by pillows, lay beneath the coverlets. Scant hair, frizzled into curls, peeped from beneath a mob cap and she wore a pair of wire-framed spectacles perched at the end of her nose as she read with slow lip movements from a large, leather-bound Bible.

A grey-haired maid twisted with rheumatism ushered James into the room and hobbled across to her mistress with his card resting upon a silver tray.

The old lady put aside her Bible and subjected the card to a close scrutiny. 'Mr Onedin? I don't think I know the name. Are you of a religious turn of mind, Mr Onedin?'

'Not particularly,' said James. 'Good afternoon, Mrs Salt. I do apologise for . . .'

She gazed at him dreamily. 'Afternoon? Is it afternoon

79

already? I keep little account of time, Mr Onedin. At my age every tick of a clock is a tiny murder. "Bring unto me my righteousness for it shall not be far off, and my salvation will not tarry". Ezekiel the prophet. He once breathed life into dry bones. Did you know that, Mr Onedin?'

'I am not wholly familiar with the passage,' James answered, politely.

Mrs Salt sighed. It sounded like the whisper of dry leaves. 'You are not a believer? I have it here . . . ' Feverishly she rustled over the pages, then abandoned the search. 'It does not matter. Many years ago my limbs turned to sticks.' Her dim, short-sighted eyes peered into the past. 'One terrible day sky and water met and brake my husband's ship into pieces. I was but eighteen and newly wed, but the sea has no mercy, Mr Onedin.'

'I am sorry,' said James gently.

'For fifty years I have searched the Testaments, but can find no context. "From him that hath not, shall be taken away . . . " My husband lived on. Died but five years ago.' She sighed again. 'He was a patient man.'

'He founded Salt Line?' asked James.

She fluttered her hand and the maid left. 'We had twenty good ships and owed no man a penny-piece.'

'And now you are reduced to a half dozen and an office that seems to do little in the way of business,' said James. 'The time is ripe to sell, before it is too late. I am prepared to make an offer.'

She shook her head. 'At my age it is no longer important.'

'Your husband devoted his life to it,' James reminded her.

'All is dust, Mr Onedin. Dust and dross.' She was as frail as a bundle of twigs and life was ebbing from her with the inevitability of a tide.

James changed tack. 'Who is Mr Sinclair?'

Mrs Salt moved restlessly. 'You must mean Lewis. My nephew. Lewis has been managing my affairs ever since my husband passed over.'

'He will bring you to ruin,' said James.

She wagged her head. 'Not me, Mr Onedin. Himself. Have you met my nephew?'

80

'Not yet,' said James.

'He has wasted his patrimony on the pleasures of the flesh. When I am gone he shall inherit the years of the locust.'

James frowned. 'It is your intention to bequeath the company to a wastrel?'

She smiled mirthlessly. 'What remains of it. Debt, Mr Onedin. A mountain of debt.'

'Let me buy you out,' James urged. 'I will give you a fair price. One which will enable you to see out your days in comfort.'

She levered herself painfully upright. 'Comfort, Mr Onedin? My only comfort will be the grave. Thank you, but no. "Those who sow the wind shall reap the whirlwind; the bud shall reap no meal: the strangers shall swallow it up." It is a small revenge, but one I find strangely nourishing.'

'I'll give you a quicker,' said James. 'Sell to me and I'll pitch him into the street.'

'That would not do at all, Mr Onedin.' She tapped the Bible. ' "As a man sows, so shall he reap." That is gospel truth and will not be gainsaid.'

She was mad, quite mad, thought James as he took his leave.

He sought out Robert. 'Sinclair can't sell, and she won't,' he told him.

'Good grief,' said Robert. 'She might live another twenty years!'

'I doubt it,' said James. He sucked thoughtfully at his teeth. 'Sinclair has accumulated a mountain of debt it seems. It bears looking into.'

He next paid a call upon Mr Gravel, his banker. Gravel, a pinched-featured man with a pair of tight-fitting, gold-framed spectacles clamped to his nose, sat at his desk in an office of Spartan simplicity. He looked up from the sheaf of documents spread before him and gazed severely at James.

'You wish to raise one and three quarter million against current assets?'

James nodded. 'That does not include projected earnings from freight. You will find those on the attached addendum.'

Gravel thumbed over the pages and studied a column of figures. 'You are anticipating an average profit of five thousand per annum, per ship?'

'Only after discounting at four per cent,' James explained. 'You will no doubt notice that I have based my calculations upon earnings over the course of the past five years.'

Gravel smiled thinly. 'Earnings are not necessarily equated with profit, Mr Onedin.'

'Mine are,' said James. 'I plough everything back, and any ship that does not pay its way is disposed of.'

Gravel considered. 'Mmmm – this Brazilian venture – it is your intention to invest all of your assets?'

'In for a penny, in for a pound,' said James. 'At the very least it is an earnest of good faith.'

Gravel pursed his lips. 'A grave risk. If it should fail . . . ?'

'You will become a ship-owner as well as a banker,' said James cheerfully.

Gravel smiled and examined his fingertips for a space of time. Then he nodded agreeably. 'I think we may be able to accommodate you, Mr Onedin. One and three quarter million at two and a half per cent.'

'Two and a quarter,' said James.

'Let us compromise at two and a half for the first million, and two and a quarter thereafter?' Gravel suggested.

James shook his head. 'Not good enough. I will compromise at two and a half and two and one eighth.'

'Done,' said Gravel. He pushed across a box of cigars. 'I might even take a flyer myself.'

'Public issue,' said James. He selected a cigar. 'And it is always useful to have a banker on the board.' He leaned forward, accepted a light, and blew out a cloud of smoke. 'By the by,' he asked conversationally, 'does Salt Line bank with you?'

'They do.' The banker poked at the end of his cigar. 'But not one of our more rewarding accounts, I am afraid.'

'Going downhill, I heard?' said James.

Gravel winced. 'It is the old story – the first generation makes the money, the second spends it. A pity, a great pity.'

James nodded sympathetically. 'From what I have heard

of Sinclair he does not impress me as the astutest of businessmen.'

Gravel glowered. 'The man is a fool.'

'Fond of the tables, I believe?'

'Gambles away the profits – such as they are – long before they come in. I tell you, Mr Onedin, were it not for Mrs Salt I would have foreclosed long ago.'

'A stubborn old lady,' said James.

'You have met her?'

'She has some strange notions,' acknowledged James.

'Sometimes,' said Gravel sadly, 'I think she is entirely bereft of reason. I have tried to advise her, but she will not listen. She has a bee in her bonnet about carrying out her late husband's wishes.'

'She is certainly a determined old lady,' agreed James. 'Just how much does Sinclair owe?'

He had thrown in the question casually, but the banker looked at him sharply. 'I am afraid I cannot give you an answer, Mr Onedin. A banker is bound by rules of discretion.' He paused reflectively. 'However, it is possible that you may find moneylenders rather more forthcoming.'

'Moneylenders?' James whistled softly. 'If the fool has run his head into that noose he'll never struggle free.'

Gravel eyed James shrewdly. 'Just what is your interest Mr Onedin?'

'Profit,' said James. 'What else?'

Elizabeth left for the office in an ill humour. She had slept fitfully, tormented by dreams of being pursued through streets of crumbling houses by a loathsome beast with the head of Albert Frazer and the body of a caterpillar. At breakfast she had discovered Grandfather Frazer already at table and looking as fit as a flea. It had taken all her powers of persuasion to dissuade him from attending upon the office in person. 'If you wrap up well, you may take a short constitutional down to the paddock and tell your troubles to Nimrod,' she had told him.

He had grumbled, and muttered that no doubt given half a chance she would put *him* out to graze with that damned horse, but had taken her advice and, driving past the paddock, she had seen Nimrod, now grey of mane and fetlocks, gazing soulfully at him as he fed the animal titbits from a capacious paper bag. The horse had snickered and pawed the ground, longing to be back in harness, as the carriage bowled along the curving driveway and out into the stream of city-bound traffic.

She arrived at her office by way of her private entrance to find Daniel Fogarty seated at her desk and hunched over the company's private ledgers.

'What the devil do you imagine you are doing?' she demanded, outraged.

He looked up and smiled affably. 'Good morning, Elizabeth. As you see, I am taking the opportunity of your tardy arrival to familiarise myself with the company's affairs.'

'By what right?' she demanded heatedly.

'The right of a shareholder,' he answered mildly.

'What?' She shook her head vehemently. 'All the money in the world wouldn't buy you into this company. This is a private concern. Our shares have never been quoted on the market.'

'You are forgetting Emma,' he said.

'Emma?'

'Frazer Shipping has been paying Emma dividends ever since old man Frazer bought out Callon Line. Emma controlled thirty per cent. She willed her entire estate to me.'

'I see,' said Elizabeth slowly. 'But you would do well to remember, Daniel Fogarty, that Grandfather Frazer has the majority holding, and if he ever learns of your involvement, those shares you hold will not be worth the paper they are written upon.'

Daniel smiled easily. 'In that case I am sure that I can rely upon your discretion.'

'You can go hang,' she snapped.

He tut-tutted. 'You really must learn to control your temper when speaking to your partner.'

'Partner!' She almost choked on the word.

'A sleeping partner for the time being. I shall play a more active role later. After we are married,' he added equivocally.

She flushed with anger. 'You take too much for granted. And furthermore, although you have lost little time in trumpeting of your wealth, no one has as yet seen the colour of your money.'

He turned over the pages of the ledgers, comparing one with the other. 'I was coming to that. Of late you seem to have been cutting your profits to the bone and even drawing upon your reserves from time to time.'

'It may have escaped your notice,' Elizabeth retorted with asperity, 'but there is a world-wide depression. The bottom has fallen out of the wheat market and we are exporting less and less in the way of manufactured goods. Shipping is a cut-throat business at the best of times. When freights are low, competition is at its fiercest.'

'My point exactly,' said Daniel, taking out his cheque book. 'What you require is a stiffening of capital. Shall we say fifty thousand?'

'Fifty thousand?' She eyed him suspiciously. 'In return for what?'

He tore out the cheque and waved it in the air to dry. 'Call it a measure of good intentions, and don't look gift horses in the mouth.'

She picked up the cheque and quickly scanned the inscription. 'I cannot possibly accept this,' she said. 'It is made out in my name.'

'I trust you not to spend it on fripperies,' he said lightly.

She replaced the cheque on the desk. 'No.'

'Really, Elizabeth, you are not thinking clearly.' He tapped the cheque. 'We could not very well put this through the company's books.' He noticed her hesitation. 'The money is to be used solely for the benefit of the Frazer Line Shipping Company. If it will ease your conscience, I will put it in writing.' Drawing a writing pad towards him he scribbled rapidly, added his signature and pushed it across to her. 'Countersign, and lodge it with your bank.'

She scrawled her signature. 'I don't know how, or when, I can repay you, Daniel.'

He grinned. 'You can make a start by dining with me. Tonight. At eight.'

Elizabeth reflected a moment, then, temperamentally unable to resist the lure of intrigue, treated Daniel to a conspiratorial smile. 'It must be somewhere discreet.'

'I know just the place,' said Daniel.

The shark-headed Captain Armstrong in brand new Captain's uniform, stepped jauntily into the street and raised his hand in a cheerful salute to Baines, marching purposefully to the office. He was rewarded with a thunderous scowl and a murderous oath as Baines plunged through the doorway and charged up the stairs.

He strode through the outer office like the wrath of God and unceremoniously flung open the door of James's private office.

'I got a bone to pick with you,' he began truculently.

James looked up from a litter of papers and turned a cold gaze upon the intruder. 'Have you not learned to knock before entering?' he asked icily.

'This is no time for ceremonials,' growled the giant. 'You have given Armstrong the *Orphir*. She's my ship.'

'So that's it?' James sighed, opened his cigar box and selected one of his long black cigars. 'The *Orphir* was never meant for you. She is stiff, cranky, a workhouse and a man-killer.' He spat off the end of his cigar and adopted a placatory tone. 'She's a young man's ship. You are too old for those games, Will.'

Baines defiantly bit off a chew of tobacco. 'Too old, am I? So I'm to be pitched on the beach, with my command given to some young stripling still wet behind the ears?'

'Armstrong,' said James mildly, 'is twenty-eight years of age and has spent the last sixteen at sea. At his age I had been master for three. It is his first command. Give the lad a chance, Will, I'll find something for you.'

Baines slewed the cud of tobacco into his cheek and spat into the fire. 'No doubt I'll be saddled with one of your toy stinkpots? Toy boats, for toy men. As senior captain first choice should be mine.'

'Lest there be any misunderstanding,' said James levelly, 'in this company the first choice is mine. My captains will take whichever ship I allocate. Or none at all.'

'I understand,' said Baines. 'Now you are rich and a power in the land, you forget old friends.'

'Don't presume too much, old friend,' said James tartly. 'I can quite understand that you want to die in harness, but when you do you are not taking an Onedin boat with you.'

Baines grunted. 'Is that your last word?'

James inspected the end of his cigar. 'No, Will, it isn't. We have been together a long time, too long to allow a simple difference of opinion to come between us. But we must face facts. None of us is growing any younger.'

'Speak for yourself,' said Baines. 'I'm as fit as ever I was.'

'Dammit, man,' said James, 'don't be so tetchy at every reference to your age. Learn to live with it as I do. You will command many an Onedin ship yet, I promise you.'

Baines snorted. 'But not the *Orphir*.'

James shook his head. 'Not the *Orphir*. She's not for you, Will.'

'Then there is no more to be said,' said Baines stiffly. He turned on his heel and was walking away, a picture of affronted dignity, when James stopped him in mid-stride.

'One moment. I haven't finished with you yet.' He unrolled a large-scale plan of his projected harbour. 'What do you think of it? The escarpment forms a natural breakwater. We dredge a channel, clear the land and use the timber for jetties, cut a road along that mountain track, bridge that chasm and run a railhead about twenty miles into the interior.'

Baines was impressed in spite of his still simmering resentment. 'It could be a fine deep water harbour for steamers. It'd take a power of dredging, mind, but once done it'll not be undone. On the other hand,' he shook his head woefully, 'it's a tidy undertaking to start a port from scratch. It will sop up money like a sponge.'

James sniffed. 'Singapore was once a swamp and Hong Kong no more than a fever-stricken island. Look at 'em now. Bursting at the seams with trade. All that was required was a mite of vision and an ounce of common sense. One day Port Baines will be the same, mark my words.'

'Port – ?' Baines stared, open-mouthed.

'Why not?' said James. 'After all, the credit of discovery belongs to you. It is the least I can do,' he added generously.

'Port Baines!' Baines's chest swelled with pride. 'Port Baines,' he repeated reverently. 'By God, it isn't every day a man has a port named after him!'

'We'll drink to that,' said James and uncorked a bottle. Baines accepted a generous tot, clinked glasses and swallowed it down at a gulp.

'To Port Baines,' said James, sipping his own drink. 'Long may it prosper.' He refilled Baines's glass.

Baines gazed ruminatively at the contents. 'I wonder who owns that interior piece?'

'Someone with an eye to business, I hope,' said James.

The following morning Elizabeth was sitting brooding unhappily at her desk when James strode in, a bundle of papers beneath his arm.

She did not want to see James, nor anyone else. Last night had been a miserable affair with one disaster following upon the heels of another. She had seen Grandfather Frazer safely tucked up in bed with a glass of warm milk, which he thoroughly detested, and, heart fluttering with excited anticipation, had slipped out of the house by a side door for her clandestine meeting with Daniel.

For a start, a drizzle of rain had been falling, then the horse had cast a shoe and there wasn't a hansom to be found for love nor money. She and Daniel had finally boarded an omnibus, conspicuous in evening dress and subject to the sniggers of their fellow passengers. They had dismounted at Castle Street and Daniel had taken her arm and guided her along a Dale Street deserted except for a few huddled groups of whining beggars and one or two hurrying passers-by crouched beneath gleaming umbrellas.

From the beginning she had half-suspected their destination and at the sight of that long-remembered, never-to-be-forgotten restaurant, her spirits had risen and in mutual accord they had quickened their pace. The windows of *Le Petit Lapin* were steamed and tears of rain trickled down the panes. Daniel had pushed open the door and ushered her inside. She had fully expected to be greeted by Henri, the same bald-headed, spade-bearded restauracuteur as so long, long ago. Instead they had been faced by a grim-faced dragon in creased black bombazine who had eyed them suspiciously before conducting them to a corner table. The restaurant had a seedy look, like a decayed gentlewoman trying to keep up appearances by primping and patching. She had wondered if it had always been so and for all these years she had been deceived by a romantic memory. Then she had intercepted a glance from Daniel. He had shaken his head sadly. 'This place has gone to the dogs. I am sorry, my dear. Perhaps we should try elsewhere?'

Wet, cold and tired, she could not have faced up to traipsing across town again, so she had summoned up a smile. 'I don't mind, Daniel. Truly I don't.' Then the waiter had appeared with a fly-speckled menu which Daniel did not trouble himself to read. 'I know exactly what we want,' he had said firmly and ordered a dozen oysters apiece, oxtail soup, a roast sucking-pig, 'and a bottle of your best champagne.'

Dear Daniel, she had thought. Like herself he had remembered every detail of that famous meal taken all those magic years ago. The waiter had paused in the act of scribbling and peered at the menu. 'We don't 'ave no sucking-pig. Never 'ave 'ad, as long as I can remember. All we got is mutton chops, beefsteak pie, rare beef, boiled mutton with caper sauce. But nothing in the way of sucking-pig. Never 'ave 'ad.'

Daniel had looked to her for confirmation and settled for beefsteak pie.

The oysters had been tough and gritty, the oxtail soup lukewarm and greasy and the pie seemed to consist of lumps of rubber baked in wet cardboard. The champagne had been warm and sticky and only succeeded in giving her an attack of hiccups.

The restaurant was stuffy and smelled of stale food. The other customers seemed to be as seedy and down-at-heel as the establishment, the gentlemen becoming more bibulous by the moment, while the ladies, bedecked in tawdry finery, screeched encouragement like so many moulting parakeets.

They had eaten their meal in unhappy silence. Daniel had paid the bill and instructed the waiter to send for a cab.

'There aren't none attainable,' the man had replied, sullenly resentful at the smallness of his tip.

'You try lambing me down, cully,' Daniel had roared in the thickest of Australian accents, 'and, so help me, I'll screw your boots off and ram 'em down your throat!'

The man had been cowed, but defiant. 'Can't leave me tables,' he had whined. 'It's more than me job's worth.' It was the obstinacy of the down-trodden, in the face of which even Daniel had to admit defeat. The waiter had exacted a small revenge for a lifetime of slurs and insults and was not about to relinquish his triumph now.

They had left with the jeers of the diners ringing in their ears and a warning from the bombazined dragon not to return, as her establishment did not cater for sight-seeing toffs. They had eventually found a cab, with a rain-sodden moke drooping between the shafts, outside a pie-stall at the bottom of Water Street. Even then it had taken the promise of a handsome bribe to persuade the jarvey to abandon the comfort of the shelter for his perch at the rear of the cab.

Then, to make matters worse, they had quarrelled on the way home. Daniel, rather tactlessly, had announced his intention, after they were married, of separating the shipyard side of the business from the shipping. It was, in fact, a perfectly rational proposal, and one she had had in mind for some time but, wretched and miserable, her one sustaining dream foundered on the rocks of change, she had flown at him in a temper. She owned a half share in the yards, handed down directly from Albert, and she had no intention of relinquishing that control to Daniel, or anyone else. Daniel took far too much for granted and she would remind him that she could have suitors galore at the raising of a finger, that he would account himself lucky if she deigned to recognise him in the street in future. There had been more in the same vein, until a second attack of hiccups had left her breathless and her storm of rage had given way to a flood of tears.

It had all been most unfair of course, and Daniel had tried to comfort her by mumbling that it was all his fault and that she should keep the yards entirely to herself if she so wished.

'You don't understand,' she had cried, weeping for the lost years. 'You don't understand.'

They had parted on terms of mutual recrimination with pride, the usurper, shouldering aside forgiveness. She had hurried back to the house with rivers of sleet falling from the sky and the trees lining the drive like restless sentinels.

She had left the house at eight and was back home and abed, and sobbing into her pillow by ten ...

Elizabeth raised her head and gazed at James with lack-lustre eyes.

'You look as though you could do with a good night's sleep,' said James cheerfully. He unrolled his plan of Port Baines and stepped back, manifestly pleased with himself as he awaited her approval.

She stared blankly at the sheet of cartridge paper. 'What is it?'

James settled himself in a chair, stretched out his long legs and explained at length.

Elizabeth listened inattentively while part of her mind brooded over her quarrel with Daniel. 'I don't understand,' she said. 'What has this wild-cat scheme to do with me?'

'Family interest,' said James comfortably. 'I thought I might let you in on the ground floor.'

'You expect me to invest good money in this nonsense? When it takes every penny I can raise simply to keep this business afloat?'

'The trade depression? Everyone is in the same boat, Elizabeth, but this venture could capitalise on that very situation.'

She frowned, perplexed by his topsy-turvy logic. 'How?'

'Once open up the interior,' said James, 'and I can fill your ships to the brim. Put up – say, twenty thousand – and we can share in the profit. Six per cent in dividends is not to be sniffed at, even these days.'

'Twenty thousand? I couldn't lay my hands on twenty thousand pence!' she exclaimed, and then remembered Daniel's fifty thousand pounds. Use it solely for the benefit of the company, he had said. 'Not a farthing,' she told James. 'All you are offering is pie-in-the-sky. All it means is that my ships will sail into your port hunting for cargoes, and pay for the privilege.'

'Not if you were to join the company as a director,' said James. 'With preferential shares and a clause giving Frazer ships favourable terms.'

Elizabeth waved a hand at his sketch plan. 'Paper. A paper port built on paper promises. No, James. I know you too well. Your schemes have a habit of lining your pockets and making beggars of others.'

James rose lazily to his feet and rolled up his plan. 'A pity,' he remarked sorrowfully. 'This undertaking will require tugs and dredgers and I had hoped that the company would place the order with Frazer's. Naturally, with a seat on the board, you would have every right to expect preferential treatment.' He winked. 'Keep it in the family, eh?'

'Family loyalty has never been one of your most outstanding virtues, James,' she retorted and then paused thoughtfully as James waited with the patience of a cat at a mousehole.

She thought again of Daniel's cheque lodged so safely in her bank, and was tempted. 'How many tugs? How many dredgers?' she asked.

'Two of each for a start,' said James. 'Single screw tugs for harbour work and a pair of bucket dredgers.'

It would, she thought, be quite a feather in her cap. Something to face Daniel with when next she saw him.

'I'll think it over,' she said. 'But I warn you, I shall require more than promises. I have no intention of paying for your tugs and dredgers out of my own pocket.'

'Staged payments,' said James. 'Ten per cent down —'

'Twenty.'

'Twelve on receipt of your cheque,' countered James.

'Fifteen,' said Elizabeth firmly.

'You drive a hard bargain,' said James. He collected the rest of his papers. 'I would like to ask a favour of you.'

'Really, James,' she said, exasperated, 'is there no end to your conniving?'

'It won't cost you a penny,' said James. 'On the contrary, I think I can promise you an entertaining evening entirely at my expense.'

'What favour?' she demanded suspiciously.

'I owe Robert a dinner,' said James mendaciously, 'and I have invited him and Sarah to dine out with me. I thought you might care to join us, that is all.'

'What favour?' she persisted.

James smiled disarmingly. 'There is someone I would like you to meet.'

Chapter Seven

Robert adjusted his tie, tugged at his waistcoat and consulted his watch. 'Five minutes of the hour,' he pronounced judiciously.

Elizabeth stifled a yawn. 'James is always punctual. It is one of his few virtues.'

'He's up to something,' said Robert darkly. 'Dinner invitations from James are as rare as snow in summertime.'

'I am sure it is most considerate of him,' Sarah contradicted severely. 'I think you do James an injustice, Robert. After all, he is our host and it is not for us to question his motives.'

'I'll feel a deal happier,' said Robert, 'when I know what lies in store.'

The three were waiting James's arrival in Robert's drawing room. It was a spacious room with lofty ceilings and wide casement windows and Robert had taken to heart Ruskin's dictum: 'Wherever you can rest, there decorate', and filled the room to overflowing with massive furniture, every inch of whose surfaces were cut, embellished, twisted and carved into grotesqueries of design. Fringed drawing-room chairs stood on gouty legs. Tête-á-tête chairs with backs like monstrous sea-shells and linked together like Siamese twins were flanked by pairs of pedestal tables cluttered with porcelain figurines and papier-mâchè boxes. A carved mahogany sofa stood on scaly legs terminating in claw feet. The marble fireplace, scrambling up the wall in a series of shelves and buttresses, had every spare inch of space crammed with knick-knacks, ornamental china, Delft-ware plates and bulbous vases. Flock wallpaper covered walls hung with vast landscapes and seascapes, prints and oleographs. It was a room which clearly stated that its possessor was a man of substance.

Sarah wore a purple dress with the skirts gathered at each side to bunch and spill over the bustle in a cascade of frills and flounces. Elizabeth had decided to honour the occasion and her mysterious admirer by dressing modishly in the very latest fashion. She wore a fish-tail skirt, tight-fitting about the lower limbs and finishing a few inches above the ankle. Above it she wore a little jacket with a stiffened basque and a white collar cut low.

Sarah pursed her lips in disapproval. 'I am aware that your taste runs to flamboyance, Elizabeth, but really, I do find that garment most immodest. Do you not agree, Robert?'

'It certainly catches the eye,' said Robert equivocally.

Elizabeth, who had chosen the dress especially to please Daniel, ran her eye insolently over Sarah's voluminous array of ruched frills and gathered folds. 'In society,' she remarked deprecatingly, 'the bustle is looked upon as *démodé* for evening wear.'

Sarah's features turned as puce as her dress. 'Not in the society in which we are accustomed to move,' she retorted sharply. 'Furthermore, as a little girl, I was taught that it was good manners never to ape one's betters.'

'Had you taken your own advice,' rejoined Elizabeth tartly, 'you would still be driving pigs to market.'

They were like two cats spitting over a bowl of cream, Robert thought, and concentrated his attention upon a minute inspection of the fringed tassels overhanging the mantelpiece.

A distant jangle of the door bell announced James's arrival. He wore full evening dress, gazed approvingly at the trio, remembered to compliment the ladies upon their attire, and hurried them away.

'Where are you taking us?' demanded Robert as they bundled into the waiting carriage.

95

'It is a surprise,' James answered blandly and would give no further information.

When the coach pulled into the kerbside the sky was clear and bright with stars and veils of fog were slowly creeping along the streets.

The basket-work at the windows alerted Robert as to their destination. 'The Cadogan!' he hissed to James. 'This is a gentleman's club!'

'It is more than that,' said James and shepherded his party into the foyer, where they were divested of their coats by a be-wigged factotum. A blackamoor in green velvet breeches and braided coat guided them along a carpeted corridor, past the smoking room, and to a thick oaken door recessed into solid masonry.

'This way,' said James and ushered them into a brightly lit room. Cut-glass chandeliers sparkled overhead. Cigar smoke drifted in waves above green baize tables. There was a low hum of voices interspersed with the click of dice and the rattle of spinning roulette wheels.

Robert and Sarah gaped. Sarah tugged at James's arm. 'James,' she whispered aghast. 'This is a gaming house!'

James gestured towards a door of studded leather. 'The dining room is through there. Excellent cuisine, I am told.'

Elizabeth, always readily adaptable to a new experience, looked about her with parted lips and glistening eyes.

The gamblers seemed to waste little time on conversation but concentrated all their attention upon the fall of a card or the last resting place of one of the roulette balls. Before each player lay piles of gold sovereigns and sheafs of banknotes. Ladies, as intent as the gentlemen, wore deep *décolleté* and were ablaze with jewels. White-gloved footmen moved quietly around carrying trays of iced champagne.

James took Elizabeth's arm. 'There he is.'

'Who?'

'Sinclair. The chap I want you to meet.'

She followed the direction of his gaze and saw a slender grey-haired man seated at a chemin-de-fer table with a growing pile of banknotes before him. Even as she watched he flipped over his cards and added fifty-odd pounds to his pile.

'Which one?' she asked, to be quite certain.

'That one,' said James. 'The fellow gambling away Salt Line assets.'

'He seems to be winning,' she said dubiously.

'Gamblers never win,' said James. 'I only wish I were his moneylender.'

'Moneylender?' Elizabeth eyed him suspiciously. 'Just what are you up to, James?'

'I want to know who holds his paper,' James told her easily.

'And what makes you think he would tell me?' she demanded, irritated at his ready assumption that she would do his bidding.

'Oh, come, Elizabeth, you know perfectly well that you can charm birds from a tree when you put your mind to it.'

'And why should I?'

'A small favour,' urged James. 'One which you may call upon me to return when the occasion arises.'

Elizabeth hesitated. 'I promise nothing.'

'You will wheedle him around your little finger,' said James confidently. 'Come along, Robert will introduce us.'

'Robert?' Her eyes widened in surprise. 'I thought you knew him?'

'Only from a photographic likeness,' said James. He nudged Robert. 'Don't stand goggling like a fish, Robert, go and make yourself known to Sinclair.'

'Card,' said Sinclair.

'Bank wins,' said the croupier, scooping in the money.

Sinclair looked up at Robert standing at his shoulder. 'Onedin? I thought my luck had changed. Are you a member?'

'I am,' said James. 'Your president put me up. Went through without a hitch.'

'And who might you be?' asked Sinclair, with eyes only for Elizabeth.

Robert hastily effected introductions. Sinclair came politely to his feet, ignored James and Sarah and took

Elizabeth's hand. 'I am delighted to make your acquaintance, Mrs Frazer. I have long held that the distaff is invariably the more attractive side of the family.'

James nodded agreeably and drifted away. Sinclair drew out a chair for Elizabeth and turned his back upon Robert and Sarah.

'Mr Frazer is not with you?' he inquired of Elizabeth.

She shook her head. 'My husband died abroad a few years ago.'

'Good for him,' said Sinclair lightly. 'Do you play?'

'What?'

'The tables.'

'I am afraid not,' Elizabeth replied coldly, concluding that this was one of the most offensive men she had ever met.

'One must never be afraid to take risks,' said Sinclair. 'Perhaps you will allow me the pleasure of instructing you?'

She looked at him quickly. He was also the most outrageous flirt imaginable. Very well, she decided, two could play at that game. She curved her lips into a smile. 'I put myself entirely in your hands,' she said and was rewarded with a veiled flicker of response.

Left to their own devices Robert and Sarah took further stock of their surroundings and timorously made their way to watch the mysteries of the roulette table. They helped themselves to free glasses of champagne, listened to the incomprehensible calls of the croupier and stared in disbelief at the heaps and piles of money passing across the table.

Robert drained his champagne and reached for a second glass. 'They must be mad,' he whispered. 'Just look at their faces. I'll warrant not one of them has done an honest day's work in his life.'

'Born with silver spoons in their mouths,' agreed Sarah.

They stood watching for a few moments longer then, as Robert was about to lead her away, Sarah impulsively opened her bag and fished out a sovereign.

'I think, perhaps, I should hazard a coin. Just one. No more. Then I can truthfully say that I have actually played this dreadful game.' She leaned over the table and placed her coin on a number chosen at random.

'Don't be foolish, Sarah,' hissed Robert. 'You are simply throwing good money away.'

Sarah shook off his restraining arm and waited, consumed with anxiety, as the croupier spun the wheel and the little ball whizzed dizzily around the outer rim before clattering into one of the slotted compartments. The croupier, a cadaverous man with tired eyes, intoned his nasal jargon and pushed a small mound of money towards Sarah.

She squealed and clapped her hands in delight. 'Robert, Robert! I've won! I've won!'

'Think yourself lucky,' said Robert sourly and tugged at her arm. Sarah feverishly counted her winnings and dropped them into her handbag. Then, after a moment's reflection, withdrew her original stake and placed it upon her lucky number.

'You'll lose,' said Robert and helped himself to another glass of champagne.

Once more the wheel spun and the little ivory ball hissed around the rim. Once again it fell into the same number.

Stunned at her success, Sarah collected her winnings. 'Just one more time,' she told Robert. 'The moment I have lost that sovereign I shall leave.'

Fascinated, she watched the spin of the wheel, but this time the wayward ball plopped into the number next to hers and she had the mortification of seeing her sovereign swept away by the croupier's rake. She fumbled in her bag. 'Just one more turn of the wheel,' said Sarah, and was lost for ever.

At the chemin-de-fer table Sinclair was regularly winning while a vexed Elizabeth was losing just as steadily.

She called for a card and turned over a six. 'Oh, damn!' she swore, rummaged in her bag and shrugged resignedly. 'At cards I am afraid I am a born loser,' she told Sinclair.

'But lucky in love, I trust?' He smiled and pushed a stack of gold coins towards her. 'You must allow me to put you in my debt.'

Elizabeth, feeling that she was getting into deep water,

shook her head. 'Thank you, but no.' She rose from the table. 'I shall borrow from my brother.'

She went in search of James and found him leaning negligently against a wall, a glass of champagne in one hand, a cigar in the other.

'James,' she said crossly. 'You owe me thirty pounds. I have lost every penny I have, while that odious creature is winning hand over fist. So much for your clever scheming!'

James took out a well-filled wallet and handed her a sheaf of banknotes. 'It was only to be expected. I have told you, Elizabeth – gamblers always lose. Keep playing. Stay with him. And use your wits.'

'It is your money,' said Elizabeth and returned to the table.

She laid the money before her and Sinclair raised an eyebrow. 'Most generous of him. And without so much as a note of hand? How very unlike an Onedin.'

Elizabeth saw her opportunity. 'What on earth is a note of hand?'

Sinclair smiled. 'My dear, you really do require instruction. Card,' he called and lost.

James sauntered across to the roulette table and found Robert angrily tugging an unwilling Sarah away from the table.

'She has lost every penny,' snarled Robert. 'And five pounds of mine into the bargain. Enough is enough, Sarah. Not a shilling more!'

'All that money!' wailed Sarah. 'I was winning, James! I was winning a fortune!'

James tut-tutted sympathetically. 'Easy come, easy go, Sarah. Come along and I will stand you both the finest dinner you have ever tasted.'

'I could not touch a morsel,' cried Sarah.

'Let it be a lesson to you,' said Robert. His eyes searched the room. 'What about Elizabeth?'

'I think Elizabeth is well able to take care of herself,' said James.

When James called, Elizabeth was having a lone breakfast.

There were dark circles around her eyes and she yawned prodigiously.

James helped himself to coffee and waited until Elizabeth had finished munching a slice of buttered toast.

'Well?' he asked.

'Well, what?' she demanded crossly. She stretched her arms and opened her mouth until her jaws were cracking. 'Lord, but I am tired. I didn't arrive home until the early hours. That man simply would not leave the table while he had a penny left in his pocket. He even borrowed fifty pounds from me.'

'From me,' corrected James. 'I hope you took his IOU.'

She shook her head. 'A verbal promise only. I was far too sleepy to care one way or the other.'

'No matter,' said James. 'Did you learn the extent of his indebtedness?'

'Of course not. There are limits, James.' Elizabeth raised a hand to her mouth and stifled a most unladylike belch.

'It can't be too high,' mused James, 'or the sharks would have closed in.' He rubbed his hands together. 'I'll pick up that company for a song.'

'But he does not own the company,' Elizabeth objected.

'Once I have the name of his usurer he won't own so much as the clothes on his back.' He helped himself to a piece of toast. 'You did obtain it, I trust?'

'I have it here.' Elizabeth fished in her pocket and handed James a slip of paper. 'He was most forthcoming. Not in the least reticent.'

James glanced at the address. 'He probably receives a commission on every client he introduces.'

'The man must be a thorough-going villain!' exclaimed Elizabeth.

'He is,' said James. 'I grant you he doesn't look the part. But if villains looked like villains the gaols would be full and only honest men would walk abroad.' He stuffed another piece of toast in his mouth and the paper into his wallet. 'And don't forget, you owe me two hundred pounds.'

She choked over a crumb. 'What!'

'A gambling debt is a debt of honour,' he told her.

deposited a brotherly kiss on her cheek and left grinning to himself before a rejoinder could leave her lips.

James found Samuel Thwaite's office by the simple expedient of mounting a flight of stairs leading from Hackins Hey and pushing open a door.

'Hullo, Thammy?' he said.

Thammy-the-note-cracker had the reputation of never forgetting a face or a debt. He was an old man, as ancient as sin, and as long as James could remember had always been old. He had a shrunken, mummified face and skin like shrivelled parchment. Only his eyes seemed alive, flickering in the face like little black snakes. He sat in a mean little office behind a mean little desk with a fire baking the room to oven heat.

'Mithter Onedin! What a thurprithe! You have remembered old Thammy after all theeth yearth!'

'I remember,' said James.

Thammy had started up in business as a note-cracker, a man who would buy a seaman's advance note at usurious rates. When signing articles a seaman would receive an advance of up to three months on his wages. Once the ship had sailed with the seaman safely aboard, Thammy would hurry around to the ship-owner's office and redeem the note. The risk was small for note-crackers and crimps worked hand-in-glove. It was the notorious blood-money system and was extended even to seamen's wives, who would cash in their allotment notes with Thammy and his ilk rather than wait a month until the note fell due.

Today Thammy had exchanged his corner table in the Bells of Glory for an office in the city while his agents handled the waterfront.

'You've come up in the world, Thammy,' said James.

Thammy shrugged deprecatingly. 'Tho have you, Mithter Onedin. I can remember the day you cracked your firtht note. You couldn't have been more than fifteen yearth of age.'

'I remember,' said James.

Thammy raised a taloned hand and combed a tuft of goat

beard. 'And in what way can I be of thervith, Mithter Onedin?'

'You have a client named Sinclair,' said James, coming straight to the point. 'How much has he borrowed?'

'Thinclair?' Thammy wagged his head sorrowfully. 'I am the victim of my own generothity, Mithter Onedin. I fear I thcuall never thee the colour of my money.'

'In that case,' said James. 'I can set your mind at rest. I am prepared to take up his notes at face value.'

'Fayth value!' Thammy raised horrified hands. 'Mithter Onedin, you cannot be theriouth! I have laid out good money . . .'

'Post-obits,' said James.

'What?'

'Lending money at exorbitant rates against the security of expectations. In this case the death of his aunt.' James shook his head. 'It won't do, Thammy. It won't do at all. I intend to buy up Salt Line. Then you can whistle for your money.'

Thammy fidgeted with alarm. 'It cannot be true! I have been athured that hith aunt will not thell.'

'She will to me,' said James, flatly.

'If Thinclair doth not pay, he will go to prithon,' protested Thammy desperately.

'For ought I care,' said James callously, 'you can throw him to the dogs.'

'It ith not fair,' wailed Thammy. 'It ith not fair, Mithter Onedin. Hith noteth are worth twelve thouthand pound, if they are worth a penny.'

James held out a hand. 'Face value, Thammy. And thank your lucky stars that I am an honest man,' he added virtuously.

Thammy tottered across the room, unlocked a deed box, scrabbled inside and fished out a thick folder. James unfastened the pink ribbon and drew out a sheaf of Sinclair's promissory notes. He spread them on the desk and carefully totalled the amount. 'I make it three thousand, five hundred,' he told Thammy and scribbled a cheque. He held it between forefinger and thumb. 'If I find that you are holding back,

Thammy, I will see to it that my company never again redeems one of your notes.'

'You are a hard man, Mithter Onedin,' said Thammy taking the cheque.

'I know,' said James, unfeelingly. 'It's a hard world.'

Mrs Salt lay propped up by a mound of pillows, her nephew's promissory notes spread before her. She turned her head. 'But this is dreadful, Mr Onedin, dreadful. Worse, far worse than I ever imagined.'

James, seated at her bedside, took one of her claw-like hands in his own. 'He will bring you to ruin, Mrs Salt,' he said gently.

She released a small dry sob. 'I was aware, of course, that Lewis had been borrowing from the bank – but to go to a moneylender . . . !'

'There will be others,' said James, 'and they will bleed him dry. For your own security you must allow me to buy you out while there is yet time.'

She sighed. 'I cannot.'

'I will tear up these notes of hand and give you enough shares in Salt Line to guarantee you a dividend of five hundred a year.'

She smiled weakly. 'Of what use are guarantees at my age? He would simply go back to the moneylenders again, and again, and again.'

'Not without security,' said James. 'And I give you my word that he will not mortgage another ship, another piece of your property, as long as he lives.'

She squeezed his hand. 'And what would you do with the company, Mr Onedin?'

'Make it pay,' James told her. 'As did your husband.'

'I believe you would.' She turned her eyes to the portrait of Captain Salt and his sightless, forbidding gaze. 'But I cannot. I gave my word, do you see?'

'I know a way,' said James.

The Salt Line offices were every whit as musty as Robert had described. James took the stairs two at a time, brushed aside the protesting arm of the greybeard, and marched purposefully into Sinclair's office.

Sinclair was seated at his desk, idling his time away by playing a game of solitaire. He looked up irritably at the interruption and addressed himself to the clerk following closely upon James's heels.

'I was under the impression that I had left strict orders that I was not to be disturbed, Mr Raven.'

James shooed out the frightened clerk and firmly closed the door. 'You have given your last order in this office, Sinclair,' he announced curtly and fanned out the collection of IOUs across the desk. 'Your credit has run out.'

Sinclair linked his · fingers together and cracked his knuckles. 'So you have been buying up my paper?' He shook his head. 'It won't do, Onedin. It won't do at all. Those notes of hand do not fall due until —'

'Until your aunt dies and you inherit,' James finished for him. 'You really are the most despicable creature I have ever had the misfortune to meet, Sinclair. A man spends a lifetime creating a business, and you throw it away across the card table.'

A flicker of temper showed in Sinclair's eyes. 'Do you imagine I enjoy this role I play? My uncle – may his soul roast in hell – hung that business around my neck like a mill-stone. I worked like a dog from dawn till night for a measly remuneration that scarce bought leather for my shoes. It was always the promise of tomorrow. "One day you will inherit," he said and dangled that bait before me until the day he died. Like a greedy fool I swallowed it. Then that mean, parsimonious, penny-pinching Gradgrind left everything to my aunt with the proviso that I would inherit only on her death. The man was a monster.'

'You are revenging yourself on the dead,' said James. 'What of the living?'

'My aunt is as bound to his resolution as am I,' said Sinclair.

'Shall we put it to the test?'

'I don't follow.' Sinclair helped himself to a pinch of snuff and trumpeted into his handkerchief.

'Resign,' said James. 'For without you there will be no Salt Line.'

'And allow you to pick up the company at bargain-basement rates? I think not.'

'I have picked it up,' said James, riffling the promissory notes. 'Only, unlike your other creditors I am not prepared to wait.'

'Other creditors?'

'Everyone to whom you owe so much as a penny piece. From your banker to your tailor. In my experience a man such as you thinks little of meeting his bills on time, if at all.'

'My dear fellow,' said Sinclair lazily, 'there is no gratification quite so costly as that of keeping out of debt.'

'In return for your resignation,' said James, 'I will foot all outstanding debts.'

'I quite fail to see,' said Sinclair, 'why I should be expected to relinquish a small, but adequate income for penury.'

'Don't teach me my business,' snapped James. 'The company is on its last legs, your ships are in a pitiful state of disrepair and, unless I am much mistaken, your masters are fleecing you blind. Don't be a fool, Sinclair, the day of judgement cannot be put off forever. Resign and you are free of a load of debt. Refuse and I shall return these notes to Thammy and he will demand his pound of flesh. I am leaving you with a roof over your head. Thammy would sell you out of house and home.'

'My aunt would never agree,' said Sinclair uncertainly.

'She will,' said James. 'She longs for escape as much as you.'

They left together and sat in silence as the carriage wound its way through the city centre and out along Prince's Boulevard to Croxteth Road and the Salt residence.

'I think she's asleep, sir,' the aged maid whispered to Sinclair and, creaking at every joint, led the way upstairs. She tapped discreetly and pushed open the door.

Mrs Salt, frizzed wig askew, sightless eyes open, lay with one arm trailing towards the floor, its hand already crooked into claws by the onset of rigor mortis.

'Oh, my God . . . !' whispered Sinclair.

The ancient maid threw her apron over her eyes, rocked to and fro and then ran from the room, her wails echoing through the house like the cries of lost souls.

James walked across and looked down upon the body. He stooped and picked up a small, fluted bottle. He shook it, sniffed the contents and replaced the stopper.

'What is it?' asked Sinclair. His voice shook and his face was clammy with perspiration.

'An empty bottle,' said James and held it up for Sinclair's inspection.

'Laudanum . . . ' Sinclair licked dry lips.

'A sedative,' said James. 'She suffered from constant pain.'

Sinclair looked piteously at James. 'She – she wouldn't . . . ?'

James carefully placed the bottle amid an array of medicine bottles. 'We shall never know,' he said. He gently drew the eyelids down over the blind eyes, closed the fallen jaw, and was settling the wig decently straight upon the balding skull, when he noticed a long brown envelope entangled with the bed covers. He picked it up, inspected the contents, then held it out to Sinclair.

'It's her Will. The company is yours, Sinclair.'

Sinclair summoned up a crooked smile. 'No, Onedin. I have lost yet again. The company is yours.'

James left him kneeling at the bedside, tears streaming down his face, and went in search of Baines.

He found that worthy resident at one of the new Sailors' Homes, which lately seemed to have been springing up like mushrooms in every seaport in the British Isles.

It was built of fresh-hewn blocks of sandstone and was strategically sited at the corner of Tar Street, behind the Customs House. A plaque set into the wall announced quite simply that this was one of the Prince Albert Foundation Homes For Sailors. Entrance was by way of a pair of wrought-iron gates fashioned to resemble lengths of rope joined at their interstices by simulated knots and seizings.

A peg-legged custodian directed James to Baines's cabin.

a small, white-painted cubicle on the first floor. The door was of oiled teak and bore a highly-polished brass knocker in the shape of a conch shell.

'Mr Onedin!' said a surprised Baines, opening the door in answer to James's knock.

'I have a job for you,' said James, taking stock of his surroundings. The room was about the size of any single-berth cabin aboard ship. There was a bunk above a chest of drawers with brass handles, a horsehair settee, an armchair with curved arms and a cane seat, a compact wash-stand. A ship's oil lamp, stationary in its gimbals, and a bookshelf containing a solitary volume of Brown's Nautical Almanac completed the furnishings. Baines, James reflected, seemed to acknowledge no other home but a ship.

'Come in,' rumbled the giant and stepped aside. 'Not the *Orphir*, I expect?' he asked hopefully.

'Not the *Orphir*,' said James. 'I want you to take charge of Salt Line.'

'Work ashore? In a office?' Baines looked affronted. 'Not me. I'm not cut out for that kind of work.'

'I have no one else,' James told him. 'You can handle ships and men —'

'Paperwork,' said Baines. 'I've no head for paperwork.'

'I have an office full of clerks who can handle that side of the business,' said James irritably. 'What I need is someone who can see to it that those ships are rigged for a North Atlantic passage. Someone who can find me first-rate masters and mates, hand-pick the crews. Someone who won't stand for fiddle-faddle. Someone to take complete charge. Hire and fire at will with no interference. There'll be a bonus in it for you.'

'I'd be shore-based,' said Baines. 'I want a deck beneath my feet.'

'And so you shall. The moment this business is settled you can take your pick.'

'Any ship?'

'Any ship available,' said James cautiously.

'It will be temporary, mind,' said Baines. 'Only temporary.'

'As you will. Just get those ships ready for sea. A crew of

six – master, mate, two ABs and two boys. Clear two of the brigs for Newfoundland with salt, then they are to run salt fish down to the West Indies and load with fruit and molasses for home. The schooners can continue carrying slate until I can find something more profitable.'

'Is that all?' asked Baines.

James missed the irony. 'For the time being.' He consulted his watch. 'I'll be on my way. If there is anything you need, ask Tupman. He'll handle the paperwork for you, and I'll have a word with Elizabeth about refitting – she has been crying poverty of late and will no doubt welcome the work.' He sniffed. 'If the price is right. Anything else?'

'I think you have about covered everything, sir,' said Baines drily.

'I see no problems,' said James. 'Pick me good crews, that is all I ask.'

'No difficulty there,' said Baines. 'I'll find 'em right here.'

'Here?'

'Prime seamen, every man-jack of 'em. Couldn't wish for better. It's these Foundation Homes, you see? New-fangled, but very go-ahead and everything in ship-shape fashion. Smart little cabins, each with its own lock on the door. The grub's good – plain but wholesome, and we got a sitting room, and a reading room and a row of shops selling everything from baccy to seaboots. We've even got a bank where a man can stow his pay until he needs it. There's a bulletin board giving information about sailing dates, which ship is opening articles and where bound. I tell you,' said Baines enthusiastically, 'these Foundation Homes are little worlds on their own. The only thing missing is a bit of salt water sloshing about.'

'Can't show much profit,' commented James. 'Who is behind it?'

Baines shrugged. 'I've no idea. But whoever they are, they seem to understand the needs of sailormen better than most.'

Leaving Baines to deal with the immediate problems, James returned to his office, outlined his proposals to Tupman, and added Salt Line to his growing number of subsidiary companies.

Later that evening, well satisfied with his day's work and replete with dumpling stew and tapioca pudding, he sat toasting his toes before the fire. Drowsily he contemplated Miss Gaunt seated opposite, busy ,with her endless sewing and stitching. Yellow tongues of flame, flickering up the chimney, sent planes of light and shadow dancing across her angular features. She was, he thought, a most reposeful woman. One in whose presence he could take quiet comfort. Comfort, he thought, drifting off to sleep. Comfort. She was a remarkably comfortable woman.

As his gentle snores punctuated the air Miss Gaunt laid her sewing in her lap and gazed dreamily into the fire. All in all she would be sorry to leave her present situation. Her employer, despite his harsh reputation, could be a most considerate person. At his insistence they invariably dined together and he had long established the practice of their sitting together, she with her work-basket, he with his newspaper, and barely a word spoken. He had, she thought, a most comfortable presence. She sighed and, raising her head, glanced up at the portrait of Anne. It seemed of a sudden to have acquired a benign look.

Chapter Eight

Sarah, seated at the lower end of the table, considered that her little dinner party was on the way to being an unqualified success. Samuel had returned from school and looked quite the little man. *So* like his father, with broad shoulders and sturdy limbs and a firm set to his chin. He was shedding his puppy fat and she would not have been one whit surprised to learn that he had been secretly shaving. Dear Samuel was as different as chalk from cheese from his cousin, William, with his saturnine looks and careful table manners. Charlotte, placed between the two boys, was becoming quite a handful, a sly young madcap who would bear careful watching. From the child's suppressed giggles and the uncomfortable squirming of the two boys, it was quite evident that she was surreptitiously pinching them beneath the table.

Sarah's eyes roved quickly over the rest of the assembled guests. Elizabeth, as was only to be expected, was making sheep's eyes at Daniel Fogarty who, for his part, looked every inch a gentleman and was keeping the table fully engaged with his account of his Australian adventures. He and Elizabeth had at first been quite distant with each other, but after such a long separation that was only to be expected. For her part Sarah was quite sure that the ice would thaw before long and the sound of wedding bells would soon be heard on the air.

There was but one small cloud smudging the horizon of Sarah's pleasure. James had quite irresponsibly insisted upon the company of the vinegar-faced Miss Gaunt. When

James had first broached the subject Sarah had readily agreed, assuming that the woman would be attending upon Charlotte in her capacity as governess and would, therefore, be dining in the servants' hall. A notion which James had immediately pooh-poohed, with the irrational explanation that the creature 'enjoyed little in the way of social life', as though the social life of a member of the servant class was of moment to anyone beyond other domestics. In vain she had protested that the last-minute inclusion of Miss Gaunt would over-balance her table-placings, send the cook into hysterics and the kitchen into chaos.

'But where can I possibly seat her?' Sarah had wailed. 'We shall be four to one side of the table and three to the other.'

'Next to me,' James had replied. And there she sat, between James and Daniel, as large as life and comporting herself as though to the manner born.

Robert, at the head of the table, had kept the wine circulating freely and the table entertained with reminiscences of the past.

'We have come a long way from small beginnings,' he was saying. 'I well remember working in father's oil shop – Elizabeth used to scrub the floors – and how she hated it!'

Elizabeth inspected her beautifully manicured hands. 'Winter was far and away the worst, and Robert was a slave-driver. I scrubbed that damned floor until my fingers were raw, but he was never satisfied.'

'You were a born lazybones,' said Robert affably. 'Always had your head in the clouds, dreaming of a life of ease.' He chuckled. 'Those were the days. Daniel was mate of a barque and rarely had two pennies to rub together . . . '

'Were you really, sir?' asked Samuel, looking at Daniel with renewed interest. 'Was she all timber, or a composite? How much canvas did she carry? What was her tonnage? How long were the voyages?'

'Do not interrupt me, Samuel,' snapped Robert.

'Sorry, Father,' said Samuel.

'I am afraid the boy is passing through a stage when he can think of nothing else but ships. His head is filled with

112

such fancies.' Robert smiled indulgently. 'When I was his age it was soldiers. I wanted to be a General, no less.'

'A more unwarlike creature than dear Robert, I cannot imagine,' cried Sarah, smiling fondly across the table.

'Oh, I don't know,' said Robert modestly. 'I reckon, even today, I could wage a better campaign than that American custard General. The Indians chopped off his head and put it in pickle, I heard.'

Sarah grimaced and put her hands over her ears. 'Really, Robert, you go too far! Not at the table, please!'

Daniel winked at Samuel. 'So you want to go to sea, do you, young man?'

'It has been my ambition ever since I can remember,' said Samuel. He stared gloomily at his plate. 'But it looks as though I am destined to serve behind the counter of a stuffy shop.'

'You thank your lucky stars that you have opportunities that were denied me,' Robert growled. 'I had to pull myself up by my bootstraps. When I first met your mother I was earning a few coppers a week, working all the hours God sends, and she was driving pigs to market.'

'No such thing!' snapped Sarah, her features beetroot-red. 'I come of good farming stock, as well you know!'

'As I remember,' interjected Elizabeth slyly, 'the Stirlings were grubbers in the soil. Clod-hoppers to a man.'

'It is true that we fell on evil times, when tenant farmers such as us were being evicted from our holdings by rapacious landlords. But at least we held our heads high, and it cannot be claimed,' Sarah added disdainfully, 'that I married for money.'

Samuel squirmed in his chair and Charlotte suddenly emitted a squeal of anger. 'He kicked me!' she shrieked. 'He kicked me, he kicked me, he kicked me!'

'That is quite enough of that, Miss,' said Miss Gaunt sharply. 'Keep your hands above the table and sit as still and quiet as a mouse, otherwise you will stand in the corner until the meal is finished.'

Charlotte scowled mutinously at Miss Gaunt's implacable face. 'It isn't fair,' she began.

'And hold your tongue,' commanded Miss Gaunt. 'We shall have no ifs-and-buts here, young lady.'

'Papa,' appealed Charlotte.

'Do as you are bid,' ordered James sternly.

Charlotte lapsed into sullen silence, William picked over the remnants on his plate and Samuel gazed uncomfortably at his knife and fork.

'If you have so much liking for ships, Samuel, why not ask permission of your Uncle James, or Aunt Elizabeth?' suggested Daniel. 'I am sure that either would be delighted to grant permission for you to visit one of their vessels.'

'But of course, Samuel,' said Elizabeth. 'I am sure that William would be only too pleased to accompany you. Wouldn't you, William?'

'No, Mama,' answered William sulkily.

'I'll give you an introduction to Captain Baines,' said James agreeably. 'He should have time on his hands for the next week or two.'

'Captain Baines himself! Would you really, Uncle?' asked Samuel, the light of hero-worship setting his face aglow. 'I say, that is most awfully splendid of you!'

'The docks are such dreadful rough places,' complained Sarah. 'One hears such awful tales.'

'Baines will see that he comes to no harm,' said James.

'I only hope he does not fill the boy's head full of nonsense,' grumbled Robert. 'Very well, Samuel, you may go tomorrow, then it is back to school with you.'

'Thank you, Father.'

'In return I shall fully expect your end of term school report to show an improvement over the last.'

'I do my best, Father, I truly do,' said Samuel earnestly. 'But I have a poor head for figures.'

'A man who cannot master figures will never master a ship of mine,' said James. 'So you listen to your father, young Samuel, and grind away at your books.'

'Take a leaf from your cousin William's book,' advised Daniel. 'William has a head like a counting machine. Isn't that so, William?'

William nodded gravely. 'In that respect I take after my father, sir.'

Sarah glanced hastily around the table and then rose to her feet. 'I think, ladies, that we should leave the gentlemen to their cigars.'

Left to themselves Daniel and James each selected a cigar while Robert lifted a decanter of port from the sideboard.

'Robert tells me that you are thinking of building a port in South America?' Daniel began conversationally.

'It is more than a thought,' said James and outlined his plans.

Daniel listened attentively while Robert passed around the port. 'An interesting proposal,' he declared at the end of James's dissertation. 'I am almost persuaded to take up a few shares, myself.'

'You could do worse than follow Elizabeth's example,' said James.

'Elizabeth? You have induced Elizabeth to put money into this venture?'

James thought he detected a quickly suppressed note of alarm in Daniel's voice. Like an animal with a life of its own, part of his brain scented danger and became alert. He needed time to think. 'We entered into an arrangement,' he said casually.

'What sort of arrangement?' This time there was no hiding the anxiety underlying his words.

'That is Elizabeth's business,' said James. 'You must ask her.' He snuffed out his cigar and came lazily to his feet. 'Perhaps we should join the ladies?'

'So soon?' Robert looked affronted. 'We have barely lit our cigars.'

'In which case,' said James smoothly, '*I* shall join the ladies,' and sauntered from the room.

'I don't understand him,' said Robert, baffled by James's demeanour. 'He has always enjoyed a cigar and a glass of port.'

'Perhaps he has an eye for that governess,' Daniel suggested lightly. Thoughtfully he tapped ash from his cigar, wondering how deeply Elizabeth was involved in James's schemes.

Robert guffawed. 'That sour-faced crocodile! She hasn't a penny to her name!'

'She has something of more value than money,' said Daniel.

'Ah,' said Robert winking lewdly.

'Character,' said Daniel.

'Of course, character,' Robert agreed hastily. 'I am sure the lady has character by the bucketful, but I doubt James has eyes for anything beyond the commodity market.'

'Money,' said Daniel. 'I was coming to that.'

In the drawing room, James, stretched out on a chair, allowed the chatter of the women to wash over him while he applied his mind to the problem of Daniel's odd attitude. From all accounts Fogarty had returned a wealthy man. He had revealed interest in the Port Baines project and as good as promised to put up capital. Why then had he shown so much concern over Elizabeth's investment? It was a puzzle, and somewhere there was a piece missing.

A hubbub, rising from behind the closed doors of the library to which the children had been banished, interrupted his thoughts.

'It sounds like a den of wild animals,' declared Sarah. 'Pray do exert your authority, Miss Gaunt, I beg of you.'

'Miss Gaunt's responsibilities start and end with Charlotte,' said James curtly. 'I'll go.'

He crossed the room and flung open the door to discover William and Samuel rolling about the floor pummelling each other's ribs while Charlotte, perched on the library table, hugged herself and kicked pantalooned legs in delight.

James hauled the two boys apart and held them wriggling at arm's length. 'Well?' he demanded. 'What is the meaning of this?'

Charlotte answered for them. 'They were fighting over me!' she squealed. 'I wanted to play knights and ladies but William said they were too grown-up so I pinched him and he was going to hit me but Samuel gave him a box on the ear instead and they have been fighting ever since.' All this

116

came out in a breathless torrent of words which only dried up as Miss Gaunt entered the room.

'Only cats and canaries perch on furniture,' said Miss Gaunt icily. 'So come down from that table this instant, young lady.'

Charlotte slithered to the floor and hung her head to gaze sulkily at the points of her shoes. Miss Gaunt stretched out an arm, took Charlotte's ear between forefinger and thumb and marched her through to the drawing room.

'You will sit there, little Miss Disgrace,' she said, dragging out a chair and turning it around to face the window. 'Put your hands in your lap, your feet together and do not move a muscle or utter so much as one word.'

'What is all the to-do?' asked Sarah, half-rising from the sofa.

'Nothing that I cannot attend to, thank you, madam,' returned Miss Gaunt stiffly and stalked back to the library.

Elizabeth grinned at Sarah's flush of discomfiture. 'It would seem our Miss Gaunt can give as good as she takes.'

James looked up at Miss Gaunt's entrance and indicated the two culprits, William dabbing at a bloodied nose and Samuel massaging a bruise over one eye. 'They are not much the worse for wear.' He pushed the pair from the room. 'Off you go and tidy yourselves up.' He sighed and pulled reflectively at his nose. 'I rather fancy that Charlotte is becoming quite a handful.'

'She is at a rather difficult age,' agreed Miss Gaunt. Privately she held the opinion that the reason for the child's tantrums and wilful behaviour could be laid at the feet of her employer, who tended to treat his daughter as an encumbrance rather than a blessing. Wisely she held her tongue.

'What she requires,' said James, 'is the company of children of her own age. I have a mind to pack her off to boarding school. This is no reflection upon your abilities, Miss Gaunt,' he added hastily. 'On the contrary I am more than pleased with Charlotte's progress over these past few months. But there it is, sooner or later the fledgling must leave home. I wonder if, of your experience, you could

117

advise of an establishment catering for young ladies of Charlotte's age and circumstances?'

Miss Gaunt's heart sank at the thought of yet once again being forced to seek a new position. It was inevitable, of course, but her present situation was of so comfortable a nature that she had buried the prospect in the recesses of her mind.

'I could recommend the Misses Childers' Academy for Young Ladies,' she answered dutifully. 'They have a most excellent reputation both in the fields of deportment and scholastic achievement, and I am given to understand that their discipline, while firm, is by no means harsh.'

'Discipline,' said James. 'That is what the child needs – discipline.'

What the child needs most, Miss Gaunt thought, is love and affection but, bowing her head submissively, she kept her own counsel.

'I shall be sorry to lose you, Miss Gaunt,' said James. He scratched his head ruefully. 'I must admit to having acquired quite a taste for your company but I am afraid there is nothing for it.'

'I quite understand, sir,' said Miss Gaunt. Her pale complexion coloured slightly. 'May I add, sir, that that is one of the nicest compliments I have ever been paid?'

James smiled. 'I find these formalities inhibiting of conversation – all these "sirs" and "Miss Gaunts" – what is your first name?'

'Letitia, sir.'

'Letitia? What does it mean?'

'It is from the Latin for gladness, I believe.'

'Gladness Gaunt!' James's smile widened into a Cheshire cat grin. 'I don't think I could manage either of those. May I have your permission to address you in future simply as Letty?'

'That is most kind of you, sir,' began Miss Gaunt.

'Well,' said James cheerfully, 'if it does nothing else it will at least wipe Sarah's eye. And you shall call me James. Agreed?'

Miss Gaunt shook her head. 'I couldn't. It would be most improper.'

'Improper?' He gave up scratching his head and tugged at an ear instead. 'Yes, I see what you mean. Tongues wag, and I am forgetting that whereas I am in a position to ignore them, you, by the nature of your calling, are not.' He transferred his hand from his ear to his chin. 'I would, however, appreciate it if you would consider dropping the "sir". It does tend to rather put us at a distance, if you follow?'

She had long learned to accept without demur the more eccentric requests of her employers, so she nodded gravely while a little bird encaged in her mind fluttered its wings and twittered an irrational song of unfulfilled yearnings.

'As you wish,' she said.

'There,' said James. 'That wasn't too difficult was it? Now we'd best join the others, else they'll think we're lost.'

He ushered her through to the drawing room where they were subjected to a battery of inquiring eyes. Daniel and Robert were comfortably settled in a couple of leather-upholstered armchairs and Robert, James noticed, looked as smug as a cat which had just swallowed a canary.

'Letty and I,' he announced, 'have just been discussing arrangements for Charlotte's future education.'

'Letty!' exclaimed Elizabeth. 'What a truly delightful name!' She made room by shuffling along to one end of the sofa. 'Do come and sit between us, Letty. There is far too much formality these days. Do you not agree, Sarah?'

Sarah squinted down her nose and wriggled to her end of the sofa as though in mortal fear of contamination. 'If it is Miss Gaunt's wish to change from the more conventional form of address I shall, naturally, not be the first to object.'

'The wish is mine,' said James flatly. 'So you'd best get used to it, Sarah.'

'Do I detect a sniff of romance in the air?' inquired Robert, winking broadly.

'No, you do not,' snapped James testily. 'It is a matter of plain convenience, that is all.' He joined the circle by plumping heavily into an armchair and lapsing into studied silence.

'I believe you were speaking of Charlotte's education, Letty?' prompted Elizabeth.

'It is Mr Onedin's wish that she furthers her tutelage by attending a boarding-out school,' said Letty.

'And what is your opinion?' asked Elizabeth. 'Or hasn't James deigned to canvass it?'

'The decision does not rest with me, Mrs Frazer,' Letty reminded her.

'Mrs Frazer! I declare I shall be quite at odds with you, Letty, unless you return the compliment by calling me Elizabeth.' She took one of Letty's hands and patted it affectionately. 'I am sure we are going to be good friends, are we not?'

'You are more than kind,' said Letty.

Daniel stifled a yawn. 'Has it occurred to anyone to inquire if Charlotte has an opinion of her own on the subject?'

Even Robert was stirred out of his torpor by this heretical view. 'The child is far too young to hold, much less express, an opinion of her own,' he protested.

Sarah nodded vehement agreement. 'Children are to be seen and not heard, speak only when they are spoken to, and are never to contradict the decisions of older and wiser heads. I am surprised that you should counsel such a thing, Daniel. You may be sure that Elizabeth never troubled to consult William before sending him off to that training ship.'

'I have it on William's own authority that he hated every moment of it,' Daniel replied mildly.

'All boys hate school. It is in their natures,' said Robert sententiously. 'Take our Samuel, for example. A finer, brighter boy you would be hard put to find. But does he appreciate the opportunities we are giving him? Not one whit. He would rather have exchanged places with William. "The grass is always greenest at the other side of the hill", I told him. "Read, mark, learn and inwardly digest. That is the purpose of schooling."'

'To read his letters home one would imagine that he had been condemned to a galley rather than one of the finest schools that money can buy,' interjected Sarah. She dabbed at her eyes and emitted a long-drawn-out sigh. 'But I have long learned that one can expect little gratitude in this world.'

'And small comfort in the next,' said Robert cheerfully. 'The boy will turn up trumps, never fear.'

'He should go down on his bended knees and thank us,' said Sarah.

James levered himself up on to one elbow and looked across at Charlotte's stiffened back. 'Very well, you can come out of purdah, Charlotte. Turn round and give us the benefit of your sentiments.'

Charlotte turned to face the group, her face set in mutinous lines. 'I won't go to a horrid school!' she cried. 'Never! And you can't make me!'

'You will need to put up a stronger argument than that,' said James.

'I shall run away!' Charlotte shouted defiantly.

'If you do, you will find your own way back, for I shan't come looking for you,' James told her calmly.

'I want to stay with Letty,' said Charlotte.

'The privilege of referring to Miss Gaunt as "Letty" is one exercised only by grown-ups,' said James. 'You will continue to address Miss Gaunt by her proper title.'

'We shall compromise,' said Miss Gaunt. 'In future you shall call me Aunt Letty. There – how will that suit?' She smiled and beckoned the child across. 'Come over here, Charlotte, and curl up on the floor beside me.'

Charlotte made her way across the room and, tucking her legs beneath her, sat on the carpet between Miss Gaunt and Elizabeth.

Miss Gaunt addressed herself to James. 'I am inclined to Mr Robert's view: young shoulders are not designed to bear old heads. If Mr Fogarty will forgive my saying so, the premise of his argument does not warrant close examination: the choice, *vis-à-vis* the young gentlemen, was of which school they should attend, not whether they should attend school at all.'

'She has you there, Daniel,' Robert grinned.

She has spirit as well as character, thought James. He looked at her features, animated with the light of argument. A sharp mind, he reflected, one quick to come to the point.

He chewed over the name. Letty. It rolled off the tongue and had a distinct flavour of independence.

'I know when I'm bested,' said Daniel easily. 'But we are no nearer a resolution of the problem: should Charlotte go to school, or no? Perhaps, Letty, you will enlighten us with your view?'

'I want to stay with Aunt Letty,' said Charlotte.

'I am sure that your Papa will make a wise decision,' said Miss Gaunt.

'Please,' begged Charlotte, tears welling in her eyes.

James gazed down at his daughter while his brain weighed the pros and cons.

'Why?' he asked.

The child's hand sought Miss Gaunt's. 'I like Aunt Letty,' she said simply.

So do I, thought James. It would be an easy solution. Give way to the child's wishes and he and Letty could continue in the same comfortable relationship. He would hate to lose her. On the other hand he was merely putting off the evil day. Charlotte would soon outgrow the need for a governess. Furthermore, she had obviously formed an attachment for her mentor, an attachment which would be the more difficult to sever with the passage of years. He made up his mind with characteristic swiftness.

'You will attend the Misses Childers' Academy for Young Ladies,' he announced.

'I hate you!' sobbed Charlotte. 'I won't go, I won't go, I won't!'

'It won't be until the beginning of the new term,' said Miss Gaunt consolingly. 'And that is years and years away yet.' If only it were, she thought unhappily. In a sense she was little different from her charge: unwanted, unloved, to be passed from hand to hand at the whim of unchallengeable authority.

'Then that settles it,' said James and lapsed into his former state of somnolent brooding.

As Samuel and William returned from bathing their wounds Daniel stood up, stretched his arms and announced that it was time they were leaving.

'Us?' inquired Elizabeth raising an eyebrow.

'I'll see you home,' said Daniel and, reaching out a hand, drew her lightly to her feet.

After they had paid due compliments to host and hostess and the door had closed behind them, James stirred from his lethargy and casually mentioned that now the Salt Line offices were in his possession he was prepared to arrive at a fair and amicable arrangement with Robert with regard to their lease.

'That will no longer be necessary,' said Robert airily. 'We shall shortly be moving to new premises.'

Sarah sat bolt upright. 'What . . . !'

'I have long held the opinion that the neighbourhood is fast deteriorating,' said Robert, 'and that a change to a new environment can only be a change for the better. With that end in view I have decided upon a choice corner site in Church Street.' He put his thumbs into the armholes of his waistcoat and sat back to survey his open-mouthed audience with an air of smug complacency.

'Church Street!' exclaimed Sarah aghast. 'We could not possibly afford it!' Church Street was at the very hub of the town shopping centre and the site values were commensurately high.

'I can now,' said Robert. 'By the by, James, you have a new landlord.'

'Who?' asked James suspiciously.

'Daniel Fogarty,' said Robert blandly.

'Fogarty?' James blinked. 'Daniel Fogarty has bought you out?'

'This very evening,' said Robert. 'Over brandy and cigars. He offered a very fair price plus an interest-free loan until such time as we are firmly established in our new premises.'

'Interest-free?' James frowned. 'Fishy. Very fishy.'

'Nothing of the sort,' Robert grunted peevishly. 'It's typical of you, James. Always looking for the fly in the ointment. It is simply that Daniel is now as rich as Croesus and does not easily forget old friends. I trust him implicitly.'

'Then more fool you,' said James. 'For loans, whether free of interest or no, have one thing in common.'

'What is that?' asked Robert.

'They deliver the borrower into the hands of his creditor,' said James.

Chapter Nine

'She's rigged as a snow,' said Baines. 'A right handy vessel, but I'm having her re-rigged as a brigantine wi' a fore-and-aft gaff mainsail and gaff topsail.'

He was conducting Samuel on a tour of the *Good Intent*, one of Salt Line's vessels lying forlornly alongside her berth in Kings dock.

She seemed, to Samuel's untrained eye, to be as busy as an ant-heap and composed almost entirely of a jumble of ropes and cordage. He ducked as a block swung dangerously near his head and promptly tripped over a deck scrubber.

'Snows is too slow to catch cold,' continued Baines, 'but as a brigantine she'll lap up the knots.'

'The *Mary Celeste* was a brigantine, wasn't she?' ventured Samuel.

Baines sniffed. 'I know what is on your mind, but it's nothing but superstitious claptrap. She was born unlucky was that ship,' he said, giving the lie to his own words. 'Her real name was the *Mary Sellars*, only some Frog painter got it wrong. I saw her once – that'd be in Boston around 1862–63. She was named the *Amazon* then. Her first captain had died on her maiden voyage, her second went bankrupt and the third ran her aground. Then her owners sold her. "Change her name, change her luck", as the saying goes, so her new owners rechristened her the *Mary Sellars* and sent her off to Genoa with a cargo of spirits. She's still afloat and still working. And she'll go on working until Davy Jones or the breakers get her.'

'It was very mysterious, though,' said Samuel.

'The sea's full of mysteries,' said Baines, 'and most of 'em are sailors' yarns, spun in the fo'c'sle for the benefit of green hands. Pay no attention, young feller-me-lad. Just take care that you never sail of a Friday, don't never whistle for a wind, always spit when you speak of the Devil, and you'll not go far wrong.'

'What sort of cargoes does the *Good Intent* carry?' asked Samuel.

'Come below and we'll run an eye over her account books,' said Baines.

In the tiny, cramped Master's cabin Baines fished out a worn, much thumbed register and watched Samuel eagerly turning over the pages. He turned back to the first page on which the crews' wages were noted. The Master, he read, was paid £5 per month; the Mate £4. 5s.; an A.B. £3. 5s.; an Ordinary Seaman £1. 15s.; and a Boy the princely sum of £1.

'Them's coastal rates,' said Baines. 'It's a mite higher for the officers when she goes deep sea, but there's few sailormen die rich.'

Samuel thumbed over a couple of pages and paused at the profit and loss account for the last voyage. 'Coal, iron, oats, pitwood, coal again, more iron, clay, bricks, slates. At the end of twelve months she has shown a profit of . . . ' He blinked incredulously. 'Only forty-two pounds, nine and tuppence?'

'She'll need to do better than that for Mr Onedin,' said Baines.

'I don't follow,' said Samuel. 'Where has all the money gone?'

'Disbursements,' said Baines, turning over the page. 'That's the catch-all. Given slack book-keeping ashore a sharp Master can soon line his pockets. Mind you, this feller was getting away with murder. According to him this ship was painted throughout twice a voyage and used more rope than a fleet of whalers. Lord, but Mr Tupman would have been down on him like a ton of bricks. I took the greatest pleasure in heaving him and his dunnage ashore. He was a

126

shifty-eyed customer and wanted to argue the toss at first.'
Baines rubbed the knuckles of one of his enormous fists and
shook his head sadly. 'But there was no spirit in the man.'

Samuel put aside the account book and for an hour sat
listening enthralled to Baines's tales of distant lands, of
storm and tempest, of iron cold and savage blizzards, of the
burning heat of the tropics, of warlike Papuans who ate
human flesh, and of peaceful Polynesians who decked
strangers with wreaths of flowers.

He eventually wended his way home with a liturgy of
place-names running through his head. *Valparaiso. The Sulu
Sea and the Torres Strait. Hokkaido and Honshu. Obidos.
Manãos. Pernambuco. Trinidad and Port of Spain. The
Windward and the Leeward Islands and the Gulf of Darien.*
He clung to the dock road until the last possible moment,
walking beneath the overhanging bowsprits of barques and
barquentines, gazing with longing at their tracery of rigging.
With every step he inhaled the rich, mingled odours of brine
and tar and hemp, and each and every step strengthened his
resolution that one day he would captain a fine ship bound
for 'Frisco round the Horn.

Reluctantly turning his back upon his dreams he crossed
the road and dawdled his way to the shop. When he arrived
dusk was falling and powdering the sky with stars. The shop
windows were already ablaze with light and a lamplighter,
his long pole balanced on one shoulder, was making his
rounds.

Inside the shop the atmosphere was stuffy and the air had
the stale taste of an overcrowded room. Stuffing his hands
in his pockets Samuel slouched gloomily through the shop,
pushed open the door to Robert's private office to find his
father, busy with scissors, paste and stiff brown paper, engaged in the construction of a passable, if rickety, model
of his new shop. He glanced up as Samuel wandered in.

'Ah, there you are, Samuel. Did you have a pleasant day?'
Without waiting for an answer he stood back and surveyed
his handiwork with a craftsman's pride. 'What do you think
of this? A bit rough-and-ready, but I venture it gives a fair
idea of development. Three storeys high – I've cut holes for

windows – three hundred foot frontage and three entrances – one in each street and one at the corner.' He stroked his moustache with sticky fingers. 'I have it in mind to put in two of the new patent elevators. What do you think?'

'Yes,' said Samuel absently. He half-listened to his father droning on about a central cash desk with an overhead railway to carry bills and money, and tableaux of wax models displaying ready-to-wear garments, while part of his mind carried him to the South Seas. *Midshipman Samuel fought fiercely, his swinging cutlass lopping off heads as the Malay pirates swarmed over the side of the gallant ship* Hector.

'A storeroom,' said Robert, 'and your mother's seamstresses can occupy the cellar. Made to Your Own Measurements. All Alterations Guaranteed within Twenty-Four hours. I think that should pull in the fashion trade. Do you not agree?'

Young Samuel and Cap'n Baines fought back to back, Samuel's cutlass flashing in the sunlight as he hewed and hacked. Samuel's sword dripped blood.

'It seems a splendid idea,' said Samuel.

'You might show a little more interest,' grumbled his father.

First Mate Samuel Onedin, lashed to the wheel, drove the ship forward in the teeth of a typhoon while the terrified crew huddled in the scuppers. 'Keep her steady, Mister Mate,' roared Cap'n Baines as mountainous seas towered high above the trestle-trees.

' . . . and there will be a small office for you next to mine.'

'Office?' Samuel came out of his dream.

'You will be leaving school at the end of term. Time to think of your future.'

'Yes, father,' said Samuel morosely.

'You will have a long, hard row to hoe, but there is no substitute for hard work. I will start you off in the stock room and then you will move from department to department under the supervision of the floor walkers. Always remember that one day you will step into my shoes.'

Samuel could not imagine a worse fate. *The ships raced neck-and-neck with the prize to the winner. 'Brace the*

128

t'gallants,' ordered Captain Samuel Onedin and, as the ship slowly crept ahead, Cap'n Baines, aboard the Charlotte Rhodes, *waved his hat in admission of defeat.*

'Don't I get a holiday?' he asked sullenly.

'Well,' said Robert jovially, 'I don't see why not. If your end-of-term report is satisfactory, I daresay we could manage a fortnight's break. What would you like to do?'

'Travel,' said Samuel. *Maranhão. The Gulf of Mexico. Suez and the Barbary Coast.*

'Manchester,' said Robert. 'You can stay with Uncle Will Perkins. A change is as good as a rest, as they say.' He gazed benignly at his son and chuckled. 'Holidays, eh? And not yet done a hand's turn. You'll be expecting to be paid for 'em next. Off with you, my boy. Wander around the store and keep your eyes and ears open. Call back at my office at closing time and we can leave together. Have a man-to-man talk, eh?'

Thus dismissed Samuel left the room, softly closing the door behind him. He would be boiled in oil before submitting to Uncle Will Perkins's regime. *Captain Samuel Onedin led his men ashore on a wild charge to relieve Cap'n Baines besieged in the Old Fort. Chimbarozo, Cotapaxi and the Skeleton Coast.*

Daniel Fogarty stood before Elizabeth's desk, shuffling and cawing like an overgrown schoolboy.

'I cannot for the life of me follow you, Daniel,' said Elizabeth. 'It is a perfectly sound business proposition. The Yards are crying out for work and James is placing a substantial order. If you are concerned about the twenty thousand pounds I have invested, I might remind you that you gave me *carte blanche* to use the money in any manner I chose, provided it was to the benefit of the company.'

'I hadn't allowed for you being ensnared in James's net,' said Daniel.

She showed a flicker of anger. 'Ensnared? Do you take me for a fool? The order for dredgers and tugs is far in excess of twenty thousand and the payments will be staged and guaranteed.'

129

'By James.'

'In business matters James may be as sharp as a weasel, but I have never known him break his word,' she rejoined tartly.

He looked harassed and ran a hand through his hair. 'If the time should come when James can't meet his commitments all the promises in the world won't be worth a jot.'

'James always meets his commitments,' she said stubbornly. 'Your twenty thousand pounds will be quite safe,' she added scornfully.

He waved a hand. 'The money is of no account.'

'It is to me.' She paused and watched him wriggling with embarrassment while the rain pattered against the windows and the fire collapsed into a shower of sparks. 'Exactly what is troubling you, Daniel?'

He drifted across the room, extended the sole of his boot and absently kicked the fire into life. 'If James's scheme goes down, he'll take you with him. That I had not planned for.'

'Planned for? Just what have you been planning, Daniel Fogarty?' she demanded suspiciously.

He turned to face her, his face twisted into an expression of long-contained anger. 'For once James has overreached himself. This is the opportunity I have been waiting for, dreamed of during all those long years of exile. I shall destroy him as he destroyed us.'

'Destroy . . . ?' Elizabeth found herself gazing at a new Daniel Fogarty. A man in the grip of an obsession. Her first thought was that he was mad. There was a glitter in his eyes, and his lips had peeled back in a tiger's grin.

'Cancel the contract, withdraw your investment, and leave me free to deal with James,' he urged.

'You deal with James?' she eyed him incredulously. 'In matters of business James will ever be your master.'

'Not this time,' said Daniel confidently.

'Daniel,' she pleaded, 'let bygones be bygones. James did what he did because Albert was his friend. It is all in the past and best forgotten.'

'*I* don't forget,' said Daniel. 'There is no escape for him this time.' He began to pace about the room. 'I have bought

130

into his companies – that way I can act as a check on his borrowings, and he'll not play ducks and drakes with their finances as long as I am a principal shareholder. I am also investing heavily in this Brazilian venture. When the time is ripe I shall bring him to his knees. And show a profit into the bargain.'

'How?'

'By artificially raising the price of all his holdings and then suddenly dumping my shares on to the market. That will effectively depress the price and force James to meet his obligations. But this time he will have put all his eggs into one basket, and when his creditors clamour for their money he will have no reserves to fall back upon.'

'Revenge,' she said. 'You are burning with revenge.'

'I'll have satisfaction,' he declared.

'And for your childish notions of satisfaction you will put paid to a scheme which will bring employment to my Yards, regenerate trade, fill our steamships with cargo? I'll have no part of it.'

'I wish you no hurt, Elizabeth,' he told her earnestly. 'I will see that you come to no harm.'

'Hurt!' she cried. 'You are filled with hurt. You bring misery wherever you go. There is no solace, nor affection, nor an ounce of kindness in you, Daniel Fogarty! You return prating of love, but your heart is set upon one goal and your eyes upon another.'

'I have but one goal, Elizabeth,' he said simply. 'You.'

'And Frazer's,' she taunted bitterly. 'Don't forget Frazer's. You have manipulated everyone – even that poor sheep Robert – and all for what? Vengeance? Or is it to salve your conscience because you drove Emma to an early grave?'

He flinched before her storm of accusations. 'That is not fair, Elizabeth. I gave up all for you, as well you know. But if possession of Frazer's means so much, I will immediately make over my shares to you.'

'So a flourish of a pen resolves all difficulties,' she said bitterly. 'Wealth has changed you, Daniel, and not for the better.'

'What would you have me do?' he asked.

131

'Abandon this madness before it comes to James's ears. For if it does, I warn you, Daniel, James will devour you like a lion a lamb.'

'Not this time,' said Daniel. 'This time I have him within my grasp. Believe me, Elizabeth, I am well able to take care of myself in the world of finance. I have learned a trick or two since I last left these shores.'

'James has been practising those tricks ever since he learned to walk,' she said contemptuously. 'Blaming him for your troubles is like blaming a fox for killing a chicken.'

He shook his head obstinately. 'I am committed. It is too late to withdraw.'

'You never did have any head for business,' she snapped crossly. 'You will find this a different kettle of fish from digging up gold and tending hordes of smelly sheep.'

Daniel summoned up a smile. 'Lions and lambs, foxes and chickens, fish and sheep. You make it sound as though we are in a barnyard rather than a shipping office.'

She was not to be drawn. 'You would do well to remember, Daniel Fogarty, that in this barnyard I am cock-o'-the-roost. I have accepted James's order and it will stand. I care not one whit for your stupid vendetta, but I do care about anything which affects Frazer's. Or have you forgotten that there are others to consider besides your own selfish ends?'

'You mean William?'

'*My* son. I am determined he shall have his inheritance in full.'

'So he shall, I promise you,' said Daniel. 'For he is my son as well, remember.'

'No. You renounced all claims to parenthood years ago.'

'That is unjust, Elizabeth,' he said quietly. 'I was at the other side of the world when your letter arrived. I drove ship and men to their limits on the return voyage, but on my home-coming what did I find but you married to that whelp Albert.'

'Albert was a good husband to me,' she declared. 'I will not have him decried.'

'More of James's machinations,' he said bitterly. 'He married you off to a shipyard, not a man.'

132

'And you married Emma Callon.' Elizabeth arched an eyebrow. 'For love?' she asked mockingly. 'Or could it be that you had an eye on a fleet of ships?'

He had the grace to look uncomfortable. 'I wronged her,' he admitted.

'You did indeed. She deserved better than you, Daniel Fogarty.'

'I know,' he agreed sombrely. 'But all that is in the past and best forgotten.'

'Then let the past bury the past,' she urged. 'Give up this nonsense and make your peace with James.'

'I shall rename the port and call it Port Isabella, Frazer ships will have first call on cargo and enter and leave free of port charges,' said Daniel firmly.

Elizabeth sighed and shook her head at the dolt. 'Very well. Be it on your own head.'

James picked up the scent of danger from Tupman. He listened attentively to the clerk's report and thoughtfully assessed his views of share activities.

'A slow but steady rise, sir,' said Tupman. 'I believe that when they top out he will sell and make a killing.'

'Fogarty,' said James.

Tupman nodded. 'Out in the open. No hiding behind nominees this time, sir.'

'Thank you, Tupman,' said James. After the clerk had bowed himself out he selected one of his long thin black cigars, put his feet up on the desk, and applied himself to the problem.

He quickly simplified it into an either-or question. Either Fogarty, backed by considerable wealth, was playing the game of bulls and bears, or he was after bigger game: control of the Brazil company. Whichever the event he was caught in a cleft stick. Sell and get out quickly and he lost the company. Hold on and Fogarty would sell, depress the market and put the Onedin companies under strong financial pressure.

James smoked two more cigars and then went in search of Elizabeth.

'He is after your blood, James,' she told him.

'Well,' said James, 'at least I know where we stand.'

'I shall never speak to him again,' she declared miserably.

'Nonsense,' said James cheerfully. 'You must not allow a business quarrel to come between you. If you are still fond of the fellow after all these years the most sensible course of action is to marry him.' He deposited a brotherly kiss on her cheek and left the office with a jaunty swing of his shoulders.

James next made his way to the office of the Brazilian Consul and emerged two hours later looking uncommonly pleased with himself.

He still had a sense of well-being when, after dinner, stretched out in his favourite fireside chair, the evening newspaper held before his face, he heard Miss Gaunt give a dry little cough.

'Ahem,' said Miss Gaunt.

This he knew to be her invariable preliminary to a conversational opening. His attention thus attracted, he lowered his newspaper and looked across politely.

For some reason she seemed ill-at-ease, moving restlessly in her chair, her hands plucking at the folds of her dress.

'Are you comfortable?' he asked solicitously.

'Yes, thank you,' she replied, then promptly contradicted herself. 'No, I am not. I mean – oh, dear – how can I put it?'

James smiled. 'Simply?' he suggested. •

She drew in a deep breath. 'I have accepted another situation,' she said quickly.

James blinked. 'Situation? What situation?'

The words came out in a rush. 'Once Charlotte is settled in her new school, it is obvious that there will be no place for me in your household, I have therefore taken the opportunity of answering one or two advertisements. I had a reply this morning. It is a position which offers most excellent prospects – a family of three young children and another on its way. Naturally I made it quite clear in my application that I would not be free to take up the appointment until the beginning of the new school term. I have been more

134

than tolerably happy in your service and my one regret is that this disclosure of my resolution may cause you discomfort.'

'I don't like it, Letty,' said James peevishly. 'No, dammit, I do not like it at all.'

'I am sorry,' she said.

He looked upon a bleak future of dining alone. Anne's portrait stared down at them with basilisk eyes. 'I am used to your presence,' he grumbled. 'I have grown comfortable with you.'

Miss Gaunt picked up her sewing. 'I, too, have enjoyed these moments of quietude. No one could wish for a kinder or more considerate employer.'

'Employer?' He shook his head. 'Not simply as an employer, I beg of you. I have come to look upon us as good friends.'

She lowered her eyes and picked absently at a stitch. 'All the more reason why I should leave,' she murmured.

James chewed at his lip and jabbed at the fire with the point of his boot. 'Do you want to leave?' he asked eventually.

'Of course not,' she replied quickly. 'But manifestly once the reason for my presence has been removed, it becomes incumbent upon me to seek new employment.' She permitted herself a lop-sided smile. 'I am afraid that transcience is one of the penalties of my calling.'

James grunted at this piece of information and lapsed into silence. 'Would you consider staying on in a different capacity?' he asked after a few moments' reflection.

Miss Gaunt shrugged her thin shoulders. 'In what capacity? You already have a most excellent housekeeper in Mrs Gibson, and I hardly see myself as a domestic.'

'Of course not. I thought, something in the nature of a – um – companion?'

She smiled again and shook her head, amused at his naïvety. 'Ladies have companions,' she said. 'Gentlemen have . . .'

'Mistresses,' James finished for her. He scratched his head

135

ruefully. 'No, that would not do. It would not do at all.'

'One must face facts,' she said resolutely. 'The problem is insoluble.'

'No problem is insoluble,' said James. 'The trick is to approach it from another angle.' He applied himself to the trick by closing his eyes, stretching out his legs and appearing to doze off. He remained in this recumbent posture for so long that Miss Gaunt was coming to the conclusion that he was fast asleep when he suddenly sat up.

'I have it!' he exclaimed jubilantly. 'It is as easy as pie! We shall get married.'

'M-m-marry . . . ?' she stammered, quite unable to believe the evidence of her ears.

'Why not?' asked James. 'It seems a most sensible solution, for we are agreed that there is no other position for you in the household — ' He broke off as she began to laugh with an undercurrent of hysteria in her voice.

'Marriage? You – you actually see marriage as the solution to a domestic problem?' Glancing down she noticed that she had run the sewing needle into her finger. She plucked it out and abstractedly licked at the blood oozing from the wound. 'I have never heard so ridiculous a proposal in my life! If it were not so amusing it would be quite hurtful.'

'Hurtful?' James looked surprised. 'I made the proposal in good faith,' he assured her earnestly, in case she had misunderstood his intentions.

'And I reject it in equal good faith,' said Miss Gaunt bridling with anger. 'If I ever should marry,' she told him coldly, 'it will be for – for . . . '

'Love?' suggested James.

'Affection at least,' she answered. 'But most certainly not as a substitute housekeeper.' With that she rose to her feet and, to James's astonishment, ran from the room weeping bitterly.

Women, thought James as the door slammed behind her, I shall never understand the creatures if I live to be a hundred. It was a pity. He had always looked upon her as a perfectly sensible woman.

He picked up his newspaper and immersed himself in the shipping news while the portrait above the fireplace looked down upon him with sorrowful eyes.

Chapter Ten

Grandfather Frazer passed away peacefully in his sleep. The frail craft in which he had navigated the final stages of his life's voyage now lay like a deserted hulk washed up on the shores of eternity.

Elizabeth gazed down at the hollow face with its sunken cheeks and slack jaw and wept bitterly. He had been a hard man but the years had softened him and his irascibility had given way to a quirky humour. She had grown fond of the old rascal and he, in his grumpy cantankerous fashion, of her. The evidence lay in her hand: a letter written in his shaky scrawl, the scribblings of a man unable to articulate the warmer sentiments. Mistily she reread the words: *Throughout my life I have made a practice of settling debts when they fall due. I owe you a debt of gratitude for no man could have wished for a better daughter-in-law.* Here the letter broke off, as though he had paused for thought, or perhaps fallen asleep. Then it resumed with a new paragraph and a new train of thought.

I have heard from many sources that that man Fogarty is back and lording it up. I cannot find it in my heart to forgive and forget and so take comfort in Scripture – But he that sinneth against me wrongeth his own soul. Proverbs Ch. 8, v. 36. So be it. Vengeance is Mine, I will repay, saith the Lord. If thine enemy thirst, give him drink. Romans Ch. 12, v. 20.

The writing disappeared into a looping, indecipherable scrawl, a sequence of jagged hieroglyphs splotched and splattered by a feverish hand as though the wandering mind had temporarily lost control. Then it continued with careful down-strokes and laboriously crossed 't's to follow a distant train of thought.

I have long been aware that you have a sentimental attach-ment for the fellow and I wish with all my heart it were otherwise. But you, and you alone, are the mistress of your affections and you, and you alone, can decide whether the currency of passion be base or true. You must therefore follow the dictates of your heart and . . . Ramble, ramble, ramble went the letter until she came to the gist of it: *You have a young life which all too soon will be wasted by the years. My advice is to marry and that quickly. Whether for love or money is of small account for both will come to the same end in the long run. It is my wish that you marry whomsoever you choose in the knowledge that my blessings go with you. My Testament remains unaltered. It is my Will and Desire that the Company be held in Trust until my grandson, William, is of age, the said Company to be ad-ministered on his behalf by you. Make your peace with*

The letter terminated abruptly and bore no date. It was as though hand and mind had finally parted company and that once indomitable will had succumbed to an even greater will than his own.

Elizabeth crumpled the letter and, pushing it into her pocket, looked down again at the recumbent figure lying in quiet repose. The marbling veins gave him the look of an effigy carved by a demonic sculptor. His head rested upon clasped hands and his knees were drawn up as though making obeisance to his Maker.

The office closed for business. Ensigns flew at half-mast. The hall table overflowed with cards of condolence and floral tributes arrived by the cartload. The household went into mourning and Elizabeth and William received a steady stream of visitors come to offer words of comfort. Obituaries and eulogistic paeans filled the pages of the *Liverpool Daily Albion*, the *Daily Post*, the *Courier* and the *Mail*. The *Shipping Gazette* carried a black-bordered tribute to the passing of one of the great captains of the shipping industry, offered tongue-in-cheek sympathy to William 'whose shoulders were too young to bear the heavy burden of responsibility' and conjectured as to the fate of the Company now that the guiding hand was no longer at the tiller.

'Once the funeral is over,' said Daniel, 'they will be snapping at your heels like a pack of wolves.'

He had kept discreetly in the background but had proved a rock of stability to which she could cling amid the shifting tides of emotion.

Elizabeth wept often, caught in the grip of a melancholia that all the tears in the world would not wash away. For all his cantankerous ways she had grown fond of the old man and now that he was gone she found herself overwhelmed with guilt and remorse. She had deceived him monstrously and would not be comforted, but would waken in the night shivering with apprehension, fully expecting Grandfather Frazer's apparition to appear waving ghostly arms and gibbering accusations, like the spirit of Caleb Greatman in *The Birthright.*

As the funeral procession passed through the town *en route* for Iron Jack Frazer's last resting-place, the shops in the leading thoroughfares closed their doors as a last mark of respect. The cortège, a quarter of a mile long, wound its way like a long black snake past the Town Hall and the Chamber of Commerce, along the dock road, past the closed gates of the shipyard with the factory hooters wailing a dirge, to its final goal, the tiny Methodist churchyard overlooking the restless waters of the Mersey.

He was laid to rest in a coffin fashioned of oak from his own yards, while the Reverend Mr Samuels, inspired by the presence of so many dignitaries, cawed his way through the burial service.

Then it was over.

James, sauntering back, held out a helping hand to a bowed figure hobbling arthritically along the gravelled path. He was a wizened old man who wore a fringe of whiskers like a muffler around a crab-apple face. James recognised him immediately as a shipowner in a small way of business. 'Good of you to come, Mr Outhwaite,' he remarked civilly.

'Ah – Onedin? Thought I recognised you.' The man sighed. 'I've come to pay my last respects. Couldn't do ought else after all these years. I daresay it will be my turn next.'

'He had a good innings,' said James ambiguously.

'Died in harness. Let it be a warning to us all.'

'You are not thinking of retiring?'

'It's a step I've been considering taking for some time,' said Outhwaite. 'The last few minutes have made up my mind for me. The grave is a cold resting-place and lies waiting for us at the end of every road, but I see little point in hastening my steps, if you take my meaning?'

'I do,' said James. 'Let me walk you to your carriage.'

Elizabeth and William received the returning mourners, who now seemed intent upon eating her out of house and home. The list of invitations had seemed endless. The more important guests had been easy to remember, the difficulty had come when sifting through the lesser lights, each of whom would be mortally offended if robbed of a lifetime's opportunity of rubbing shoulders with the great. Elizabeth had resolved part of the problem by first assuring Mr Dunwoody, her Chief Clerk, that it had been Mr Frazer's expressed wish that he should attend the funeral and that she, for her part, would be desolated if he did not join the other invitees for a small repast; then she begged of him the favour of his choosing from among the work force those whom he considered worthy to attend. Dunwoody had considered it an honour and a privilege and had applied himself assiduously to his task – the results of his endeavours now standing in a corner, a nervous congregation of thick-soled, shiny boots and serge suits.

Elizabeth had thrown open the dining room, library and drawing room, through which, like water finding its own level, the tidal flow of guests had surged into a series of backwaters. Baines, new boots squeaking at every move, stood towering above a covey of ships' captains; Robert held sway over a circle of business acquaintances; Sarah, cocooned in black and swathed in veiling, was enthroned in the drawing room where she reigned over a clucking of matrons; Charlotte and a band of pigtailed playmates had found their way into the garden and were whooping noisily and indecorously outside.

Elizabeth, picking her way through the gossiping groups, noticed that the once lugubrious faces and muted tones had gradually been superseded by an air of conviviality, and that conversation was now punctuated by short bursts of laughter. She discovered a bored-looking Daniel engaged in conversation with Letty Gaunt and the Reverend Mr Samuels. Taking his arm she drew him aside.

'I do wish they would leave,' she whispered crossly. 'It is beginning to sound more like a bear-garden than a funeral.'

Daniel grinned down at her. 'You have been too generous with the food and drink. Turn off the tap and they'll soon be making their excuses.'

She watched a couple of portly burghers helping themselves liberally from the sideboard and summoned up a smile. 'Well, at least no one can say that we haven't given him a good send-off.'

'We could improve the shining hour,' said Daniel. He nodded towards the Reverend Mr Samuels nibbling like a mouse upon a dry biscuit. 'We could approach the reverend gentleman with a view to putting up the banns, if you have a mind for it.'

He spoke banteringly, but it was obvious that serious intent lay behind his words and she longed to say, 'Yes, yes, Daniel, let us marry now, even before a congregation of mourners.' Instead she tried to look affronted and failed hopelessly. 'I shall require a more romantic proposal than that,' she said and found her mouth curving into a smile.

'When?' he asked, pursuing his advantage.

She considered: 'There must first be a reasonable period of mourning' – and suddenly realised that she had accepted him.

Daniel nodded gravely. 'And in the meantime?'

Elizabeth smiled. 'You must pay court to me.'

'Agreed.' He gave her arm an effectionate squeeze. 'I shall be your true Galahad.'

Elizabeth could play this game for ever. She gave him an

142

answering hug. 'I hope not. I never cared for a man of such stainless character. I prefer Don Juan.'

'I cannot pretend to his list of conquests,' said Daniel, entering into the spirit of the game, 'but I promise to challenge him for the greatest prize of all.'

They could, she felt, have continued this delightful exchange for hours but she had her duties as hostess to consider. She disengaged herself and drifted contentedly from one thronged room to another, each overflowing with suddenly delightful people, until she reached the library which the gentlemen of substance seemed to be using as a smoking room. The air was thick with the blue fumes of a dozen or more cigars and through its haze Elizabeth could just make out the figure of James talking earnestly to a shrunken goblin with a furze of whiskers about his face.

She returned to the drawing room to discover that the first movements of a general exodus were taking place. Mr Dunwoody, his egg-shaped head gleaming with perspiration, was busily shepherding his flock towards the hall doors, while Daniel played the part of host to the shuffling queue of departing guests.

Miss Gaunt called Charlotte from the garden and the game of hide-and-seek amid the shrubbery came to an abrupt end. Robert shook hands with the last of his party, helped himself to a final glass of Madeira, collected Sarah, remembered to thank Elizabeth for her hospitality, mumbled that he doubted they would see his like again, and headed unsteadily for his waiting carriage.

By the time the hall clock had chimed four, doling out the hours as though unwilling to loosen its grasp of time, the last of the mourners had departed and Elizabeth was left alone with Daniel and William. She sank gratefully into a chair, kicked off her shoes and wriggled her toes. 'What a day! I think William bore himself very well, don't you, Daniel?'

'Remarkably well for one so young in years,' Daniel agreed. 'You are to be congratulated, William.'

'Thank you, Uncle,' said William. His dark eyes gazed speculatively at Daniel. 'Are you really my uncle?'

'Just an honorary one,' answered Daniel lightly.

'I wondered,' said William. 'For I can find no trace of any Fogartys in the family.'

Daniel grinned. 'Been tracking me down, have you, son?'

'Just curiosity,' said William.

'If you don't fancy the title,' said Daniel casually. 'You might care to consider "father".'

Elizabeth's heart gave a thump and she sat still and quiet, mouth dry and incapable of uttering a word.

'I half suspected it,' said William gravely.

Even Daniel seemed taken aback at this frank admission. 'You did?'

'Well,' said William judiciously, 'it was rather obvious, wouldn't you say? I mean, neither of you are particularly good at keeping secrets.'

Elizabeth found her tongue at last. 'You – you know? And you don't mind?'

'Why should I?' William smiled. 'After all, it is your affair. Privately, I consider it an excellent match. I hope,' he added warmly, 'that I may be the first to congratulate you both?' He pumped Daniel warmly by the hand. 'I daresay "father" will take a bit of getting used to, but no doubt given practice, I shall manage.' He released Daniel's arm, went to his mother and deposited an affectionate kiss upon her cheek. 'I wish you all the happiness in the world, Mother,' he said and stepped back, obviously mightily pleased with his astuteness.

'Thank you, William,' said Elizabeth shakily.

'I think,' said Daniel, expelling a long-held breath, 'that this calls for a celebration.'

'Loch Linnhe,' said James. *Snip, snip, snip*, went the scissors. 'A train to Glasgow, then on to Fort William,' he continued, flicking over the pages of the Bradshaw.

Letty, leaning across the table, readjusted the pattern. *Snip, snip, snip, SNIP*, went the scissors.

'It will be an outing for Charlotte,' said James loudly. He sighed. He seemed to be making little headway. 'Naturally, you will accompany her.'

'As you wish,' said Letty and *SNIP, snip, snip, snip, snip,* went the scissors.

'It is an overnight train so we shall take the sleeper. Change at Glasgow.'

Snip, snip, snip, snip, snap.

'Then we board the local for Fort William.'

Clickerty-click, clickerty-click.

'It will be Charlotte's last opportunity of acquainting herself with the countryside. I believe that the Scottish Highlands are noted for their scenic beauty and, as the train passes through places of historical interest, the journey should also prove to be of educational value.' James began to realise that he was speaking like one of the more stilted passages from a Baedeker. He sighed again. Miss Gaunt did seem to be in one of her more intractable moods these days. He could only suppose that he had offended the woman in some way. Presumably it had been his well-meant proposal of marriage, although for the life of him he could not understand why such a commonsensible solution to a problem should have in any way discommoded any reasonable person.

'It is very difficult,' said James, 'carrying on a conversation with a pair of scissors.'

Clack, clack, clack, clack.

Letty laid the scissors aside and smiled stiffly. 'I beg your pardon, sir, I am afraid I was not paying full attention.'

James frowned. There was that damned 'sir' again. She seemed to have armoured herself with a shell of politeness: a shell into which she would retreat at the slightest hint of apprehension. He was unused to being placed at a disadvantage and found the role decidedly uncomfortable. There were times when, with conversation at a premium, he felt that he was walking on eggshells. This, it seemed, was one of those times and he wondered yet again what on earth it was that ailed the woman.

Miss Gaunt, for her part, felt increasingly uncomfortable in his presence and privately cursed herself for a fool. He had made no further overtures after that first idiotic proposal and her equally idiotic refusal but had continued the

145

even tenor of his ways as though nothing had changed their relationship. A second opportunity would never present itself for he had assuredly accepted her decision as that of a rational woman. The situation was absurd. She found herself pulled this way and that, one moment wishing with all her heart that she could turn back the clock, the next looking forward to the day when she could leave the household for ever and put an end to this maddening, perplexing situation. There was also the increasing warmth of her feelings to take into account, for lately she had found that she could barely look in his direction without blushing furiously. At night, lying abed in the solitude of her room, wild imaginings would rise to torment her mind. Marriage and the mysteries of the flesh haunted her sleep. She had taken to examining her features in the mirror, searching for blemishes and the tell-tale wrinkles of age. She was twenty-nine years of age, condemned to spinsterhood and a lifetime of caring for other people's children.

'On the other hand,' James was saying, 'we could take the shorter route to Oban. What is your opinion, Letty?'

The continued use of the familiar rather than the more formal locution invariably had the effect of making her heart trip like a tiny hammer. 'I have no opinion on the matter,' she replied, forcing herself to drop the 'sir' and wishing she had accepted his invitation to call him by his forename. 'I have never visited Scotland and am therefore quite unfamiliar with the Western Highlands.'

'Then it shall be the long way round,' said James affably. 'It should be quite an adventure for you.'

Adventure, she thought: if only it could turn out so; and for a moment she wondered what possible motive he could have in taking Charlotte to so remote a wilderness.

'Business,' said James as though reading her thoughts. 'But I see no reason why business should not be mixed with pleasure on occasion. We shall pack a hamper and take a supply of travelling rugs, for I understand that the Great North of Scotland Railway is still in the Puffing Billy stage of development.'

'I am quite looking forward to it.' Miss Gaunt brightened

at the prospect of the three of them being closeted together for the greater part of the journey.

'Wait until you get there,' said James mysteriously. 'I have quite a surprise in store.'

The Midland Railway Company had recently introduced American-style Pullman coaches on its Scottish service. Additionally, for the greater comfort of its passengers, it had also converted one or two coaches into separate sleeping compartments. It was into one of these tiny cabins that Letty and an excited Charlotte retired for the night while James took himself off for a last cigar before returning to the gentlemen's section.

Charlotte, who had plagued her father with questions throughout the day, and received nothing but enigmatic replies in return, fell asleep immediately.

Miss Gaunt, on the other hand, lay awake for a full hour, listening to the *dub-a-dub, dub-a-dub-dub* of the wheels and the occasional shrill scream of the steam whistle as the train roared through the night. *James*, she thought. Such a dear name. *James and Letty*, they went together like bread and butter. *Bread-and-butter, bread-and-butter, bread-and-butter* sang the wheels, clipperty-clopping over the points and bellowing through darkened stations. *Bread-and-butter, bread-and-butter, bread-and-butter* echoed her mind. She had never travelled in such luxury in her life. That her employer could well afford it was unchallengeable, but he was not a man who indulged himself in the more sybaritic pleasures – on the contrary he tended to live a somewhat Spartan life; and yet they had dined off roast pheasant accompanied by a bottle of claret, their hamper was stuffed with good things and they were travelling first class.

She drifted off to sleep, well content, her head a little muzzy from wine and with a little worm of curiosity burrowing into her subconscious. James never embarked on the simplest project without planning every step of the way. What, then, could be his purpose in insisting that both herself and Charlotte should accompany him on a business trip to some outlandish place she knew only from history books?

'Charlotte!' she said and awoke to a grey dawn and the clatter and clank of the train pulling in to Glasgow Central.

James bribed a porter to take care of their baggage and they breakfasted off kippers and brown bread and butter at the railway hotel before taking the local train to Fort William.

In contrast to the luxury of the Pullman this train offered cold comfort. The coaches were small and flimsy, the seats hard, the windows grimy, the compartments isolated from each other, the entire caravanserai being towed by a rusted tank locomotive with a chimney like an old-fashioned top hat, an open-air cab for driver and fireman and an enormous brass dome hissing and spitting steam.

After leaving the environs of Glasgow the train skirted Loch Long, shuffled its way past Loch Lomond and, panting and wheezing, puffed its way through the Grampians before grinding and snorting into the Highlands proper.

The shining black rails ran like a river between towering snow-capped mountains whose flanks were clothed in brown bracken and purple heather. Hills rolled away from wide glens speckled with sheep. Streams rushed down the mountain-sides to join swollen rivers splashing and gurgling beneath stone bridges. The train puffed and panted; stopped at small wayside stations as though gathering its breath for the next stage of its journey.

The scenery grew even more rugged and spectacular as they circled Rannoch Moor, ran beside Loch Trieg sparkling in the sun and emerged at Glen Spear and the Braes o' Lochaber. Charlotte scurried from one side of the compartment to the other, her nose glued to the windows, crowing with wonder as each new vista unfolded before her eyes. Even James and Miss Gaunt were caught by the child's enthusiasm and, when James took down the hamper, unbuckled the straps and produced a repast of baked ham and cold chicken with fresh-baked bread and a bottle of cool white wine, they at last found their tongues and broke through the barrier of constraint.

By the time they had passed Inverlochy Castle and chugged into Fort William nestling beneath the towering height of Ben Nevis, Miss Gaunt had come to the conclusion that this had been the happiest day of her life.

They stayed at a three-storey hotel, grim-faced and built of weathered granite, but with the advantage of overlooking the tiny harbour at the northern end of Loch Linnhe.

'The steamer is not due until tomorrow,' said James, and refusing to answer further questions, busied himself with a writing pad and a block of telegraph forms.

Miss Gaunt and Charlotte changed from their travelling costumes and set off for a brisk walk along the quay. The town was little more than a fishing hamlet stretched along the shoreline, but at a wooden pier jutting out into the calm waters of the loch Miss Gaunt discovered a weather-beaten notice board which announced that the paddle steamer *Jupiter* would be sailing for Oban at nine the following morning.

They retraced their steps, sauntering past a row of shops at one of which Miss Gaunt bought a tam-o'-shanter for Charlotte and a plaid shawl for herself. The sky was blue, the air crisp and clear and the narrow cobbled streets ran like frozen rivers down to the water's edge. High above the roof-tops Ben Nevis raised his bald head and growled across the glens. Sheep grazed over land upon which General Monk's fort had once stood. The rounded towers of Inverlochy Castle brooded over all.

Charlotte clutched Miss Gaunt's hand and skipped along the pavement. 'It's lovely!' she cried. 'I could live here for ever and ever!' She performed a small hop, skip and a jump. 'I wonder,' she mused aloud, 'what can possibly be the special surprise Papa has promised?'

Miss Gaunt had been exercising her mind with the same question. A journey by steamer? To Oban? What could possibly await them at Oban? Which, from a close study of a gazetteer, seemed to be little other than a tiny fishing port at the mouth of Loch Linnhe.

She smiled at Charlotte. 'We must wait and see, little Miss Curiosity.'

Baines opened the telegraph form and frowned in perplexity. 'I'm to report at Oban,' he told Peg-leg Bates, the gnarled custodian of the Sailors' Home. 'With best top hat and frock coat, it says. What d'ye make of that?'

'I dunno,' said Peg-leg. 'But if I was you I'd haul my wind and shake out a reef or two. From all accounts, I hear your Mr Onedin is not the kind of man who likes to be kept waiting.'

Chapter Eleven

The *Jupiter* was painted green with a long black funnel, a straight stem and a yacht-like ornamental stern. Her paddle boxes, forward of the funnel, were inset into the hull and linked by a broad bridge. She had steam up and was puffing placidly at the pier as she waited for the last of her motley collection of passengers to troop aboard.

There were not many: a couple of shepherds wrapped in plaids and raw from the wind of the glens, with a parcel of new-shorn sheep; shawled fishwives with baskets of fresh salmon and salted herrings; a squad of red-coated, kilted soldiers in the charge of a giant corporal; a dozen or so staid families with squalls of skirmishing children running about the decks; a dominie with a forbidding gaze and a severe-looking wife.

James, Letty and Charlotte had boarded the vessel early and occupied a couple of staterooms in the first class accommodation, aft.

We really are quite the little family, thought Letty, as they ventured on to deck at the first jangle of the ship's telegraphs. The journey thus far had proved a most exciting adventure and James had added to her pleasure by showing her every kindness and consideration to such an extent that she had at last overcome her initial shyness and now addressed him as 'James'. A fact which seemed to fill him with secret amusement.

As they stood on the raised upper deck watching the activities of the seamen casting off lines and hauling them inboard, he linked her arm in a most familiar way as though they had been boon companions for years and spoke of the advantages of paddles over screw propellers in narrow inland waterways. 'She is powered by a steeple engine and a haystack boiler and the paddles can work either in tandem or separately,' he explained, and she thought this gibberish the most splendid of poetic imaginings that could be desired.

She jumped as the starboard paddle suddenly thundered into reverse, thrashing the water into a welter of foam, and she found herself suddenly hugging his arm the closer. For a moment she imagined that she felt an answering pressure but, stealing a glance at his features, detected nothing but a look of professional interest in the manoeuvring of the vessel. Then Charlotte, not to be outdone, linked her other arm and broke the magic of the moment with her incessant chatter until the port paddles began to revolve and flail the water like a giant egg-beater.

The *Jupiter* moved out into mid-stream, then, with both paddles churning as one, her funnel belching clouds of gritty black smoke, set course for Oban. A cool wind laden with the balm of heather rippled the waters of the loch and blew the smoke ahead of the ship where it waved like mourning veils and sent the lower class passengers hurrying for cover. Astern a flotilla of fishing vessels bobbed and curtsied in the widening wake and at either side the mountains of Nevis and Ardgour slid past in a slow-moving panorama.

James raised his head and sniffed the air. 'A nor'-easter,' he pronounced. 'It will bring snow.'

'Oh, surely not,' said Letty. 'There isn't a cloud in the sky.'

'There soon will be,' said James prophetically.

They promenaded arm-in-arm around the deck for a few minutes, then James sent Charlotte off to count the number of paddles to each wheel while he and Letty settled into a pair of deck chairs.

They sat in comfortable silence for a while, listening to the chunk of the paddles, the steady beat of the engine and the wild skirling of the ever-present black-headed gulls. The sun was warm, the air fragrant, the motion of the vessel as gentle as that of a fireside rocking-chair. Letty closed her eyes and allowed her imagination to drift and bob like a cork on an ocean of dreams.

'Romantic enough for you?' asked James softly.

She came out of her reverie and clasped his hand as though it were the most natural thing in the world. 'Oh, yes, James,' she breathed. 'It's lovely. I don't know how I can ever repay you.'

'You could make a start,' said James gravely, 'by abandoning all thought of seeking a new appointment.'

'I could not,' she answered confused. 'I mean . . . ' She trailed off miserably as the cloud lurking just beyond the horizon of her contentment suddenly loomed, dark and heavy with foreboding.

'*I* mean,' said James levelly, 'that my offer still stands.'

'Offer – ?'

'Of marriage.' James smiled. 'It has taken a deal of planning to arrive at this point. I hope I am not about to be disappointed a second time?'

Her eyes widened and she caught her breath. Surely he could not be in earnest?

'On the former occasion,' continued James, 'you may remember implying that you favoured something a little more romantic in the way of a proposal. I had intended to wait until tomorrow, but . . . ' He waved a hand expansively towards the rugged grandeur of the scenery slowly drifting past. 'I think this should meet the case.'

She began to laugh until her eyes welled with tears. 'Oh, James, James, you dear, demented fool – will you never change? Will you always manipulate people and circumstances to your own ends?'

'We are what we are,' said James stiffly. 'I take it, then, that you refuse?'

Letty snuffled and mopped at her eyes. 'What woman could possibly refuse so gallant a proposal? Of course I accept, you foolish man. How could I do other?'

'Good,' said James. 'Then that is settled.' He eyed her fondly. 'I am sure we shall be quite comfortable together.'

They disembarked at Oban promptly at one o'clock with the heads of the surrounding mountains already wrapped in cloud and the first flurries of snow whipping down the narrow streets.

'It won't last,' said James as the pony and trap carried them to their hotel. 'It will have blown itself out by to-morrow.'

The *Jupiter* gave a farewell tootle on her whistle as she headed out for the Firth of Lorne and the final stage of her journey round to Glasgow. Letty craned her neck and watched the steamer rounding the headland until, paddles thumping, plumes of smoke pouring from the funnel, a squall of snow blotted her from view. The last she heard was the faint bleating of sheep punctuated by the throaty whistle of an approaching train.

'That should be Baines,' James announced cryptically as the trap drew up outside an hotel all turrets and gables.

'Captain Baines?' she repeated, silently praying that James would not allow the mundane world of business to intrude into her idyll.

'He has been idling his time too long in Liverpool,' said James, handing her down to the pavement. 'I have work for him up here.'

In the foyer her hopes that James could put business aside for one more blessed day were quickly dashed for no sooner had he signed the register, arranged for their baggage to be sent to their rooms and ordered lunch for one-thirty, than he excused himself and hurried across to join a group of three men seated about an open log fire.

The trio rose at James's approach and shook hands politely. One was a tubby little man with a freckled face and a thatch of thinning red hair. He clutched a satchel of documents and spoke with the soft, lilting diction of the Highlands. 'Everything is in order, Mr Onedin,' Letty heard him say. 'Just one or two papers that require your signature then the transfer will be completed.'

The other two bore the stamp of seafarers the world over. Each wore workaday serge, clumsy boots, and moved as though they expected the floor to roll beneath their feet.

One was a short, stocky young man with a broken nose and tattoo marks on the backs of both hands. The other was bearded like a latter-day Moses and spoke with the unmistakable sing-song accents of Wales. 'By Cadwallader, but it is indeed a privilege to make your acquaintance, Mr Onedin,' he was saying as Letty and Charlotte made their way upstairs. 'I look forward to welcoming you aboard, sir.'

His voice drifted away and the conversation became no more than a low murmur as Letty and Charlotte followed the porter around the angle of the corridor leading to their room.

When they returned Letty found that the group had disappeared, their place now taken by Baines, his massive bulk wedged into one of the fireside chairs, a glass of malt whisky grasped in an enormous paw.

He came to his feet and beamed down at her. 'I understand congratulations are in order?' He put his hands to her shoulders and held her at arm's length. 'You certainly got yourself a prize here, Mr 'nedin. Pretty as a picture and as smart as they come.'

'Thank you Captain Baines,' smiled Letty. 'That is one of the nicest compliments I have ever been paid.'

He released his grip, bent down, and scooping Charlotte up, held her high in the crook of one arm. 'Well, young lady, and what do you think of your new Mama?'

Charlotte kicked her legs. 'I think it's lovely, we shall be together for ever and ever and I shan't need to go to that horrid school, will I, Papa?'

'That,' said James, 'is entirely dependent upon your good behaviour.'

'When I'm a grown-up,' said Charlotte, 'I shall do as I please and abolish all schools.'

Baines gave her a bear-like hug and deposited her on the floor. 'When you are grown-up I shall marry you and we'll sail away to the land of sugar-plums and candy.' He picked up his glass and drained the contents at a gulp. 'Best thing that ever come out of Scotland. A drop o' good hooch, that.'

'You will be staying to lunch, Captain?' asked Letty politely.

'No, ma'am, thank you kindly. There are things to be took care of,' Baines replied and, to her surprise, closed one eye in a knowing wink.

'Off you go,' said James – somewhat brusquely, she thought – 'we'll meet at nine sharp, tomorrow morning.'

'At your service,' said Baines, winked broadly again and rolled out into the street.

James took Letty's arm and escorted her to the dining room. 'By-the-by,' he said casually as he took out his napkin. 'I trust you are in favour of a quiet wedding?'

'Oh, yes, indeed,' she said, her mind buzzing with thoughts of a trousseau. 'The quieter, the better. I hate fuss.'

'Good,' said James. 'I am glad we are of a like mind. I believe I can accommodate your wishes.'

The morning dawned bright and clear with a warm sun turning the fallen snow to slush and setting the roofs to dripping with fronds of ice.

After breakfast they met Baines in the foyer. 'I've got a parcel of scallywags for you,' he told James without preamble. 'They're a sorry lot, but the best I could manage at short notice.'

'We'll soon lick 'em into shape,' said James. 'A short voyage breaks hearts and pays no wages.' He led the way to a pony and trap waiting outside, the Shetland pony as tough and hardy as the land from which it came, the driver a raw-boned Scot, slow of speech and with but a limited command of English.

'They are heathens,' said Baines, settling himself in a corner of the hard bench seat. 'Heathens to a man, living in a heathen country and speaking a heathen tongue.' His whisky-laden breath filled the crystal-clear air. 'But they brew whisky better than the devil himself.'

They left Oban behind and plodded up a narrow, rutted track until they reached a tiny plateau tufted with wind-worn grass and wild heather. Dismounting, they climbed a knoll of loose stones and a tangle of bracken.

Baines swept Charlotte up into his arms and Letty caught her breath at the view. The waters of Loch Linnhe, sparkling beneath the sun, stretched away to the north and east, bordered by hills clothed in snow and dotted with the sails of foraging vessels. The long, low-lying island of Lismore lay fringed with surf guarding the entrance to the Sound of Mull opposite. She swayed in the keening wind and looked down. The township of Oban clung like a huddle of toy buildings clustered about the shoreline with its wave-lashed jetty lapping a tiny bay. A half-mile opposite the snow-clad hills of Kerrera Island frowned down upon the narrow Sound.

James held her arm and pointed down. 'There – what do you think of them?'

Far below, anchored in the bay, lay two deep-sea sailing ships as alike as two peas in a pod. She thought them the most beautiful sight she had ever seen. Of long, slender lines with raked masts, gracefully curved cutwaters and rounded sterns, they were painted white over all and the sun flashed from the polished brasswork of stanchions, skylights, capstans and binnacles. The furled sails were frogged with snow and snow lay in a white carpet over hatch covers and decks. They looked, Letty thought, like a pair of toy ships made of sugar.

'Beautiful,' she whispered as though afraid of breaking the spell.

'That is the *Neptune* lying just ahead of the *Trident*,' said James. 'Would you like to go aboard?'

'Can I?' She had never set foot aboard anything larger than the *Jupiter* in her life.

James smiled. 'I don't see why not, they both belong to me. I settled the details yesterday afternoon. I bought them from a Liverpool shipowner who was winding up his affairs prior to retiring.'

Letty gripped his arm the tighter. One surprise seemed to follow another with this remarkable man. 'Shall we be putting to sea?' she asked.

'Of course,' said James. 'Idle ships cost money and those two have been laid up long enough. The *Trident* is Llewellyn's ship, the *Neptune* Captain Baines's.'

'A saucy vessel,' declared Baines. 'As sweet as you could

wish to find. I'll give Llewellyn a run for his money.'

'You won't,' said James. 'I have already telegraphed our Liverpool office. The *Trident* is to sail at noon and load for Valparaiso. Llewellyn has his orders. I have other plans for you.'

'Ah,' said Baines, once again winking broadly. 'A frock coat and top hat job, eh?'

James consulted his watch. 'He should be heaving up at any moment now.'

Even as he spoke Letty saw a scurry of ant-like creatures moving about the ship. Some were clambering up the masts and swinging out along the yards, while others had shipped the capstan bars and were tramping a circle through the snow. Their voices came faintly over the air, ringing and echoing from the sides of the surrounding hills, as they chanted to a slow rhythm:

> *Was ye never down Mobile Bay,*
> *Screwing cotton all the day,*
> *Where a dollar a day is a white man's pay,*
> *Riding on a donkey?*

Letty could just make out the figure of the bearded Moses standing straddle-legged on the poop. He waved grasshopper arms and the fore topsail shook out and filled amid a flurry of powdery snow. She could hear the rattle of the yards, a counter-song from those straining at halyards, bawled orders; then more sails broke out, the ship eased forward, the figures around the capstan moved more quickly; there came the steady clank of the anchor cable through the hawse pipe; then the anchor itself, gleaming wet and dripping from the depths; more sails bloomed, the ship turned and heeled and, with twin arrows of foam cleaving from its stem, headed out through the narrows, reaching for the open waters of the Firth of Lorne.

'Very smart,' said Baines approvingly. 'Only thing is, he should've turned the hands to afore breakfast and swept them decks clear of snow. Clear decks make for clear working.'

They watched the departing ship as it bore round on a

south-westerly course and, with the nor'-easter behind her, crowded on all sail and sped for the open sea.

Baines sighed. 'That old Welshman is as smart as a whip and he's kept his crew.' He looked reproachfully at James. 'While all I got is a parcel of curmudgeons. Off-scourings, the dregs of Glasgow.'

'Her Owner paid them off,' said James. 'But Llewellyn stuck to his guns and refused to part with a man-jack. Said he would pay for them out of his own pocket first.'

'Ah, well,' said Baines philosophically. 'At least I've got a hardcase Mate; between us we'll knock some sense into 'em.'

They returned to the hotel, collected their baggage and made their way to the quay where a waiting coble took them out to the *Neptune*.

Charlotte scampered first up the lowered companion-ladder and crowed with delight the moment she set foot on deck. Letty followed more staidly to be greeted by the beefy, broken-nosed young man she had last seen at the hotel.

'Mr McArdle, our First Mate,' said Baines introducing them.

'I am well pleased to make your acquaintance, ma'am,' said Mr McArdle in a marked Glaswegian accent.

'He's a Scot,' said Baines affably. 'And like all his country-men speaks as though he is chewing a mouthful of broken glass.'

McArdle grinned amiably. 'Och, it's no worse than some Sassenachs I have heard, Mistress Gaunt. I have sailed with crews where the port watch canna understand a word of the starboard.'

As their baggage was swayed aboard and James paid off the boatmen, Letty took stock of her surroundings. The decks had been swept clear although a few patches of snow remained, dripping in icy runnels from hatch covers and standing rigging. The three raked masts rose to dizzy heights and the sails were neatly furled on crossed yards. The deck was of oak and all other woodwork of teak and mahogany and so beautifully fashioned as to bear comparison with the work of the finest of cabinet-makers. Even to her inexperi-

159

enced eye the ship seemed to be of perfect proportion and balance with a look of delicate, almost fragile, beauty.

The crew, however, idling about the deck, were as ragged a group of scarecrows as she had ever set eyes upon. Some were bare-footed, some wore pairs of down-at-heel boots; all were dressed in a motley collection of threadbare garments which varied from torn and patched shirts to out-at-elbows jerseys.

'They're a sorry lot,' said Baines, following the direction of her glance. 'But with a short voyage they can't have a dip into the slop chest. Their only hope of salvation is to pray for fine weather.'

Letty had always thought of Captain Baines as a warm-hearted man, but it seemed she was mistaken, for now he was in his natural element it was evident that he was as heartless as a plantation slave-driver. The ship, too, for all its grace, must be a heartless place to these poor wretches.

'This is your steward, ma'am,' said McArdle. He beckoned with a forefinger and a wizened, sparrow-like man hopped forward and stood hovering over the baggage, his ancient, lined features creased into a grin of welcome.

'Signed for a sailor, didn't you, Billy-boy?' asked Baines.

The man hopped from one foot to another and knuckled his forehead. 'Aye, Cap'n.'

'Then this should be a soft berth for you,' said Baines. 'You take good care of the lady, d'ye hear?'

'Aye, Cap'n.'

'Because if you don't, I'll hang you out to dry. D'ye understand me, old man?' growled Baines.

The steward seemed not in the least put out by the threat. He grinned perkily at Letty. 'He's a real fire-eater, inn't he?' He picked up a couple of pieces of baggage as easily as though they were filled with feathers. 'If you will follow me, lady?'

He led the way to a door beneath the long poop deck, down a flight of carpeted stairs, along a short corridor with stateroom doors at either side and ushered Letty into a wide cabin with brass-rimmed portholes, chintz curtains and white bulkhead panels delicately bordered with azure and vermilion. There was a brass bedstead, a plush sofa and a reclining chair, a small table covered with a brocaded cloth, a marble wash-stand and a small private water closet. Letty thought it quite the prettiest room she had ever seen.

Billy-boy set down her baggage and stood, hands on hips, gaping around admiringly. 'Do 'emselves proud, does the after-guard,' he said. 'I've never been this far aft before. Not below, that is.' He wiped his nose on the back of his hand. 'This is me first berth as a steward, but I daresay I'll pick up the how of it as I go along. Been a sailorman all me life, now I've come down to this. Cap'n Baines seems to think he's obliging me with a favour on account of I'm not so young as I was. But I'm as spry as a chicken and I can still reef a tops'l wi' the best of 'em. I've no taste for stewarding, and that's a fact, ma'am, but I'm tidy in me habits so you'll have little cause for complaint, I promise you.'

Letty took a liking to the garrulous old turkey. 'I am sure I shan't, Mr – ?'

'Williams, ma'am. Billy Williams. On'y everyone calls me Billy-boy 'cos I'm a mite stunted in me growth.'

Letty smiled reassurance. 'Service must not be confused with servility, Mr Williams. I have spent my life in the service of others, but I assure you that I find nothing demeaning about my work. It is a profession like any other and to succeed in it requires the same assiduous application of skill and industry as you would apply to your everyday tasks as a seaman. If your calling is that of steward, then aim to be the best steward available.'

Billy-boy mulled over her advice, then brightened as distant vistas opened up before him. 'I could take a berth on one of them steamers filled to the gunwales wi' rich passengers. I've come across passenger-boat stewards wi' more airs and graces than a Lord Mayor. I'll practice on you, lady, and you can tell me where I go wrong.'

'The first thing,' said Letty, fishing in her bag, 'is to accept your tip.' She handed him a half-sovereign and watched him staring in disbelief at the gold coin nestling in the palm of a calloused hand.

'I dunno what to say. It's too much. I mean, all I've done is hump a couple o' bags.'

'It is common practice,' Letty told him. 'An earnest of good faith on both sides. If, at the end of the voyage, your conduct has proved satisfactory, you receive another one.'

'Start my eyes!' he ejaculated. 'It's money for old rope! You and me are going to get along famous, lady.' He pocketed the coin and rubbed his hands together. 'Now then, what can I do for you?'

'I would love a cup of tea,' said Letty.

'No sooner said, than done,' said Billy-boy. 'And if there is anything else you fancy, just give a jangle of the bell. I'll be in me pantry,' he added with a proprietorial air.

Left to herself, Letty unpacked to the sound of the tramp of bare feet above, hoarse commands, the squeak of block and tackle and distant voices raised in ragged unmusical refrain as their owners announced to the world at large that they were bound for the Rio Grande.

She was looking through one of the portholes, watching the land slowly cavorting past as the ship swung and edged forward to ease the strain on the anchor cable, when Billy-boy returned carrying a tray upon which stood a steaming mug of tea and a plate of sweet biscuits.

'It's fresh from the pot and I stirred in a fair measure o' conny-onny and a lump or two o' sugar.' He looked on expectantly as she took a tentative sip at the muddy brown liquid. It was hot, undeniably sweet, and strong enough to melt the spoon which he had considerately left sticking out of the cup.

'I hope it's to your liking?' he asked anxiously. 'Maybe I should've let it stew a bit longer?'

'Thank you,' she said. 'It will do very nicely.'

Once he had left she poured away the contents and made her way up on deck and joined James and Baines on the poop.

The anchor was already swinging from the cat-head, the jib flapping and banging in the breeze. The topsails filled as the yards were braced round. Then the *Neptune* picked up speed and bore away for the castellated tower of Duart Point lighthouse.

Letty stood in fascinated silence, absorbed in watching the activities of the seamen and only occasionally sparing a glance towards the looming bulk of the island of Mull. Some of the sailors, she noticed, worked with practised skill, others were clumsy and seemed ill-adapted to shipboard life and required pushing and shoving into place by an evil-tempered Mr McArdle. Some, in answer to barked commands, ran aloft like sure-footed cats, while others clung fearfully to shrouds and ratlines. The more experienced seamen lay out along the yards and cast off gaskets and buntlines while their fellows below hauled away on sheets and braces. The lower courses boomed and roared in the wind, the ship heeled and then settled into her stride.

'They're like a bunch of washerwomen,' said Baines disgustedly. 'Hardly a true sailorman among 'em.' He leaned over the rail and bawled down at a group of men straining at the forecourse lee braces. 'Put your backs into it, you dozy, idle parcel o' longshoremen! Mr McArdle – liven 'em up there!'

It was a brutal life, she thought, and wondered why men should hazard themselves to such barbarous treatment. Then, as the *Neptune* passed through the narrow waters separating Mull from Lismore island, she became vaguely aware that they were heading in a quite different direction from that taken by the *Trident*.

She plucked at James's sleeve. 'Where are we going?' she asked.

He smiled down and put an arm about her shoulders. 'On a voyage of discovery. Have you ever visited the Western Isles?'

She shook her head. 'No, never.'

He led her to one side out of earshot of the others. 'If you are agreeable,' he said, 'we could spend our honeymoon cruising the islands.'

She had been watching Charlotte leaning over the stern rail while she threw pieces of bread to the circling clamour of gulls, and at first the import of his words escaped her.

'What – ?' Her hand flew to her throat. 'Honeymoon – ? But – I don't understand – ?'

'Would that be romantic enough for you?' he asked with a glint of humour in his eyes.

'Romantic?' Her eyes widened and the breath caught in her throat. 'Oh, James . . . ! If only it could be so! But – how . . . ?'

'Everything has been arranged,' said James.

They were married standing on the poop, with the crew as congregation and Mr McArdle and Billy-boy as witnesses.

A zephyr of wind plucked at her skirts as the ship sailed through the Sound of Mull and Captain Baines, in new top hat and frock coat, intoned: *'Forasmuch as James and Letitia have consented together in holy wedlock, and have witnessed the same before God and this company, and thereto have given and pledged their troth either to the other, and have declared the same by the giving and receiving of a ring, and by joining hands: I pronounce that they be man and wife together.* And I wish you both all the happiness in the world, and permission to broach the rum, sir?'

Chapter Twelve

'Betrothed?' Sarah's normally sallow features took on a rosy flush of excitement. 'What splendid news! I am so happy for you both!'

Elizabeth held out her hand upon which sparkled her engagement ring, a many-faceted emerald surrounded by a cluster of diamonds. 'Only a formality, really, but Daniel insisted.'

Daniel smiled fondly at Elizabeth. 'We shall be putting up the banns on Sunday.'

Sarah frowned at the information and pursed her lips. 'So soon after the bereavement? You will forgive my saying so, Daniel, but there are times when I think Elizabeth has no sense of the proprieties. Do you not agree, Robert?'

The four were taking tea in Sarah's drawing room. A fire smoked quietly in the grate and rays from the pale April sun leaned into the room and glinted from the brass fireirons.

Robert, who had taken up a stance before the fireplace, was not to be drawn. He cleared his throat and hrrrmphed importantly. 'I think, my dear, we can leave that problem with the Reverend Mr Magnus.'

'No problem there,' said Daniel. 'A donation to his restoration fund easily assuaged his conscience.'

Robert was never one to lose an opportunity. 'I believe this calls for a celebratory toast,' he announced firmly and, avoiding Sarah's frosty stare, hastened across to the sideboard.

'Actually, I came to beg a favour of you, Robert,' said Daniel.

'Anything,' said Robert, busily pouring. 'Anything at all. Just name it.'

'I would very much appreciate it,' said Daniel, 'if you would consent to act as my groomsman.'

'Groomsman? My dear Daniel, I would account it a privilege,' replied Robert warmly and adding an extra measure to his own glass.

'And I,' said Elizabeth, 'have come to beg a similar favour from you, Sarah. Would you be my matron of honour?'

'My dearest Elizabeth,' gushed Sarah, 'I should be most affronted if you so much as dreamed of considering anyone else.' She wrapped arms like tendrils about Elizabeth and gave her an affectionate squeeze. 'You may safely leave all the details to me. First, there is the question of the reception . . .'

'We had thought of a quiet wedding,' said Daniel. 'Just family.'

'You can put that idea out of your head,' said Robert jovially as he handed round drinks. 'The groom has no say in the matter, as I know to my cost.'

'We were as poor as church mice,' said Sarah. 'But dear Robert did not stint himself. We had a wedding cake . . .'

'And Sarah had baked a ham and we managed to share a bottle of claret between us.'

'It went quite to my head,' said Sarah archly.

Robert took a gulp of his whisky. 'I think we should hold the reception here.' He beamed at their surprised faces. 'Why not? We have ample accommodation. Bride and groom can change into their travelling costumes in one of the guest rooms, and we have a large garden going to waste. We could erect a marquee and serve champagne.' He blew through his moustache and tucked his thumbs into the armholes of his waistcoat. 'I shall claim the groomsman's privilege of standing the cost.'

'That is most generous of you, Robert,' said Daniel, pumping him by the hand.

'Oh, Robert, you dear, dear man,' cried Elizabeth and

deposited a sisterly kiss upon his side-whiskers.

Sarah nodded vigorously, her earlier strictures forgotten at the prospect of being hostess to what she was determined would be the wedding of the season. 'A most excellent suggestion, Robert. We must make provision for about a hundred guests. Now whom should we invite . . . ?'

'A hundred?' said Robert aghast and beginning to count the cost.

'Certainly not less,' said Sarah firmly. 'We have our position in society to consider. One must be *extremely* careful on these occasions not to give offence by omission.'

Daniel exchanged commiserating glances with Elizabeth and shrugged resignedly. 'So be it, we shall leave everything to you, Sarah. But if it is to be so grand an affair you must allow me to share some of the burden, Robert.'

Robert was tempted, but knowing on which side his bread was buttered, managed to summon up a weak smile. 'Wouldn't dream of it,' he protested. 'After all, one good turn deserves another, eh, Daniel?'

'Yes,' said Daniel thoughtfully. 'I am obliged to you, Robert.'

'First things first,' said Sarah practically. 'Who shall head the guest list?'

'James, I suppose,' said Robert glumly. 'Although I would not put it past him to arrive trailing that governess at his coat-tails.'

'She seems a pleasant little body,' said Elizabeth. 'Perhaps we should extend an invitation to her.'

'A governess!' wailed Sarah. 'At my reception!'

'It is *my* reception and *my* wedding,' Elizabeth reminded her sharply. 'I shall invite whom I choose.'

'Yes, yes,' interposed Robert hastily. 'But that always presupposes that James is back in time.' He scratched his head. 'I wonder where the devil he is?'

The *Neptune* creamed her way through waters green and placid and disturbed only by the wavering shadows of the rocky amphitheatre of Loch Scavaig.

They had spent a blissful fortnight sailing between the

islands of the Inner Hebrides and finished by circumnavigating the Isle of Skye. The weather had been kind, the scenery breathtaking and in the Inner Sound Baines had seized the opportunity of putting the ship through her paces. Blooming with pyramids of white sails, her white reflection mirrored in the pellucid sea, the *Neptune* had flown like a white bird between the islands of Raasay and Rona and the red sandstone outcrops of the mainland.

Then, rounding the northernmost point, they had swept into the Little Minch and sighted the bare, wind-blasted heaths of the Outer Hebrides, a rocky shield held against the onslaught of the wild Atlantic.

Under topsails, jib and spanker the *Neptune* nosed her way into the narrow entrance to Loch Coruisk above which towered the black slabs of the Cuillins.

Baines ordered the fore and main topsails clewed up, put the helm down, hauled down the jib and waved his arms at the Mate to let go the anchor. As the chain rattled through the hawse pipe and the ship lost headway, Baines turned to James and beamed with self-gratification. 'All snugged down, sir. She's as lively a vessel as I ever set foot on. Twelve knots sharp on a bowline and given a fair wind I reckon I could crack on fifteen or sixteen.'

'Better than the *Orphir*?' asked James slyly.

'That old tub?' replied Baines scornfully. 'The *Neptune* would run rings round her.'

'Well,' said James, 'I promised you the ship of your choice, so the decision rests with you.'

'I'll take her,' said Baines promptly. He sighed. 'In many ways she reminds me of the old *Pampero*. Now there was a ship to take the eye. As sweet a vessel as you could find. Poor old lady, now she's naught but bleached bones lying on the beach at Tierra del Fuego.' He dolefully shook his massive head. 'I doubt I'll ever forgive myself. I chanced my arm once too often.'

'It's in the past,' said James. 'Think to the future. Once we arrive in Liverpool you will be loading and clearing for the West Indies.' He grinned a trifle self-consciously. 'For the present you will oblige me by breaking out the jolly boat.

I have a fancy for taking my new wife ashore.'

Letty was busily helping Billy-boy to pack a hamper. He had lost much of his initial clumsiness and, under Letty's tuition, had learned to cut sandwiches into neat triangles rather than the enormous doorsteps he at first favoured. She had also taught him to lay a table with the correct assortment of knives and forks and to set out a tea tray with pots of tea, cups and saucers and side plates. She had then badgered Baines into supplying him with a steward's jacket and a clean pair of white duck trousers from the ship's slop chest. Billy-boy had responded by shaving daily, washing the grime from his hands, and by following her about like an adoring spaniel.

'This is the life,' he said, handing her a couple of napkins. 'Warm and snug and pickings from the cabin fare for me stummick. I on'y wisht I'd thought of it afore. All them wasted years, freezin' aloft and at the mercy of every bucko mate who has a notion to break your head, when I could've been laying aft and living the life of Riley.'

The kicks, cuffs and curses meted out to the crew were the one side of shipboard life that Letty found disturbing. 'Is all that bullying really necessary?' she asked.

'Aye, Missus, it is,' Billy-boy told her. 'You get all kinds shipping in the fo'c'sle. Preachers and sojers, clod-hoppers and gypsies, and not a man among 'em would willingly lay out along a yard, no matter how nicely you asked him.' He shrugged his thin shoulders philosophically. 'Can't be helped. It's the way o' the world.'

'It is a cruel way,' said Letty.

'Aye, Missus, it is, but it's the on'y one we got.' Bill-boy stepped back and gazed admiringly at the neatly laid out hamper. 'You got a real talent for everything ship-shape. Neat as apple pie, I call that. Couldn't have done better meself.'

Letty smiled as she buckled the straps of the hamper. 'I am sure you will make an excellent steward, Mr Williams.'

'Thanks to you, Missus.' He picked up the hamper. 'I'm looking forward to stretching me legs ashore.'

Letty called for Charlotte and the child, who now had

Letty's stateroom entirely to herself, came running. She wore a print frock, pantaloons, white cotton stockings and a cape. In one hand she clutched her favourite doll, a goggle-eyed sawdust grotesque with fuzzy yellow hair whom she had christened Thelma after her best friend. She had been on her best behaviour, explored every nook and cranny of the ship, pestered Baines with childish questions and rapidly became a favourite of the crew.

'I am quite ready, Mama,' she told Letty, having adapted herself to the new relationship with unquestioning acceptance of the vagaries of the adult world.

Letty settled Charlotte's straw bonnet more firmly upon her head and led the way on deck where James awaited them, slowly pacing the poop as he smoked a cigar and engaged Baines in conversation. He had dressed for the occasion by wearing a deer-stalker's hat, purchased in Oban, tweed trousers and a check-patterned great-coat. He threw away the stub of his cigar when they arrived and ushered them along the main deck and down the companion-ladder to the waiting jolly boat.

The jolly boat carried four oars and, skimming over the surface, soon grounded its bows upon the shingle beach. While one of the crew carried the painter ashore and made it fast to an upturned oar, James led his party along a winding path which climbed to a plateau of tufted grass.

Here, sheltered from the high winds by the jagged peaks of the surrounding Cuillins, they lunched off cold bacon and boiled eggs with Billy-boy fussing over them like a mother hen.

A sense of drowsy contentment stole over Letty and she lay back, basking in the warm sun, her thoughts a patchwork of languorous memories. She became aware of James stretching out beside her and, peeping through slitted lids, fondly watched him tilt his hat over his eyes and settle into an attitude of repose. Beyond him she could just make out the figure of Billy-boy repacking the hamper and a whisk of movement that was Charlotte chasing a butterfly.

She closed her eyes again and drifted off to sleep to be awakened by a shrill wailing scream, a nightmarish howl of terror that raised the hairs on the nape of her neck. She sat up quickly as James, also awakened from his slumbers, uncoiled his length and came to his feet.

She stood beside him and, shading her eyes, gazed around the plateau. To the south was the winding path sloping down to the loch where the ship lay, its reflection dancing in the ruffled waters. The wind soughed and whimpered across spurs of black rock which, jutting into the tableland, made caves of darkness impenetrable to the eye. On the plateau only the hamper remained as mute testimony to the presence of Charlotte and Billy-boy.

James and Letty stood looking at each other, heads cocked, listening for a repetition of that unearthly howl.

Then a voice called: 'Ahoy there! Topside, ahoy!'

'Billy-boy,' said James. He cupped his hands. 'Where away?'

'Down here,' answered the voice. 'But watch your step, it's treacherous.'

'This way,' said James and set off at a run.

The plateau wound around the shoulder of a hill and suddenly they found themselves with a yawning gap beneath their feet. Here some cataclysmic upheaval had riven the plateau into a series of clefts and gulches.

The voice called again from somewhere beneath their feet: 'Ahoy, topside! Topside, ahoy! Look out below!'

They looked down, deep down into the rounded bowl of a corrie. Hemmed in by steep black rocks, it fell away into a jumble of boulders and the glint of water. The precipitous sides, fissured and seamed, rose in jagged perpendicular spires from an abyss of eternal night. A few circling sea birds, shrilling and shrieking, had made their nests in cracks and crevices and upon the outcrops of grass-green ledges.

It was upon one of these ledges that Charlotte lay, face downward, one leg buckled beneath her, her frightened whimpers stirring the birds into flurries of beating wings. Then they espied Billy-boy. He was clinging like a spider to the sheer wall of cliff, hands and feet carefully seeking for cracks and crevices as he slowly made his way down to the ledge.

'We are here, Billy-boy,' called James softly.

'Aye, aye,' said Billy-boy and continued his perilous downward journey.

Once, his foot slipped and a dislodged stone clattered to the depths below, leaving him clinging to the rock face at the full stretch of his arms, before his scrabbling foot found a safer toehold. He moved crab-wise, easing his way along until he came to a short buttress, pitted and scarred by the weather. Its base terminated at the ledge and the watchers above held their united breaths as he angled outward to slither down the last few feet.

He teetered for one heart-stopping moment, then dropped to one knee beside Charlotte. They saw the child twitching and shuddering as she stretched out thin arms to clutch desperately at her rescuer's knees.

'There, there, my lovely,' they heard him say. 'Don't look up and don't look down. There's naught to be afeared of now your uncle Billy-boy is here.' He looked up and called: 'A twisted ankle, but no bones broken. She's got a touch of the vertigos, is all.'

'Stay where you are,' James called down. 'I'll fetch help. You wait here,' he told Letty and set off at a gallop.

She nodded dumbly and remained, stomach churning and heart beating madly, staring down at the two figures perched so precariously on the narrow ledge. It lay about fifty feet below the lip of the corrie at the bottom of which, as her eyes accustomed themselves to the gloom, she could make out a tarn of water and up-thrusting pinnacles of needle-like rock. Her head swam dizzily and she had a vision of the child's body turning over and over like a falling leaf until it impaled itself upon one of the sharp spears.

'We'll be all right, missus,' called Billy-boy reassuringly. 'You step back a pace or two – 't'aint safe at the edge.'

Letty did as she was bid and lowered herself shakily to the grass where, with bitter bile rising to her throat, she remained to rock herself to and fro in folded arms.

In twenty minutes James returned at the head of the panting boat crew. They had stripped the jolly boat of oars and lugsail and its twenty-fathom length of painter. They set to work quickly and soon, with the minimum of fuss, had erected makeshift sheer-legs from the lugsail spars and an oar. A block was secured to the point of intersection and the painter quickly rove through.

James took the free end and his hands dexterously formed it into a bowline on a bight, while he privately thanked a merciful Providence for prompting Baines to make up the boat crew from the pick of the seamen. He thought for a moment, then opened the lay of the rope and rove through a short length of line which he fashioned into a pair of handcuffs. Now even if Charlotte fainted she would be held in place.

'Under below,' he called and tossed the end down.

Billy-boy caught the line, hauled down until he had sufficient play, then called up: 'Hold it!'

James peering over the top signalled the hands tailing on to the line and waited until, far below, Billy-boy had gently eased the twin nooses of the bowline over Charlotte's legs and slipped her wrists through the makeshift cuffs.

'Take the strain,' he ordered. 'Easy. Easy now.'

The rope tightened, pulling Charlotte into an upright position.

'Hold it,' called Billy-boy.

As the rope taughtened the seamen ceased hauling, easily holding the weight of Charlotte's body.

Billy-boy talked to her softly. 'It's no more than swings and roundabouts,' he said. 'You're going to have a nice ride up in a bos'n's chair. You can't slip and you can't fall, so you be a good girl and do as you're told. All you got to remember is to push your legs out against the rock.'

'I can't,' she wailed. 'My leg hurts.'

'Do your best,' said Billy-boy, 'and be brave.' He waved an arm to James above. 'Haul away handsomely. Handsomely does it.'

James circled his hand to the seamen who began to haul steadily, hand-over-hand. The block creaked and squeaked as the line tightened and the lignum-vitae sheave began to revolve about its brass bush.

The terror-stricken Charlotte swung like a tiny pendulum,

twisting and turning at the end of the rope, bumping and bruising her back against the rough surface of the rock face.

Then her head appeared over the top and James dragged her to safety, held her in his arms, hugged and crooned, then carried her away from the nightmare to lay her gently upon the grass and leave her to Letty's administrations.

They lowered the end again and Billy-boy, settling himself into the loops of the bowline, kicked out against the face of the rock and came up in a series of leaps and bounds. He kicked at the edge as his face came level and swung on to the knoll of grass with the agility of a monkey.

'I owe you a service,' said James, pumping him warmly by the hand.

Billy-boy grinned sheepishly and scratched his head. 'It warn't nothing special. No worse than going aloft in a bit of a bluster.'

'You'll want for nothing,' said James.

'Well,' said Billy-boy, 'I've developed a taste for steward-ing and, if you could see your way to it, I'd be eternal grate-ful to make it permanent.'

'I'll do better than that,' said James. 'From this moment on you will sail as chief steward, with chief steward's pay, chief steward's perks and a pension at the end of it.'

While a couple of the hands dismantled the sheer-legs the others made a temporary stretcher from the lugsail and a couple of oars. Charlotte was trembling and shivering from shock as she was laid gently in the stretcher and the caval-cade set off on their return journey to the cove and the waiting boat.

'She'd took herself off exploring while youse was having a quiet nap,' Billy-boy explained. 'So I thought I'd best keep an eye on her. Never thought she'd come to no harm, I just wanted to be sure she didn't wander off and get herself lost. I never dreamed there'd be a dirty great 'ole there; the first I knew was when she let out a yell and fell over the edge. When I looked down it didn't half turn me stummick, I thought she was a gonner for sure. Providence must've put that ledge there and it's another miracle that no bones was broken.'

'Amen to that,' said Letty devoutly.

James scooped Charlotte up in his arms and carried her up the companion-ladder. In answer to Baines's mute inquiry he simply snapped: 'Heave up and get under way. Set course for Liverpool and crowd on all sail. Drive her, Baines, drive her.'

He carried the child below and laid her tenderly on her bed, then, while Letty undressed her, hurried away to fetch the medicine chest.

They soon found that Billy-boy's report of Charlotte's injuries had erred on the side of optimism. The knee of her right leg was painfully swollen, she had cracked a couple of ribs and her right ankle was twisted at an unnatural angle.

'Dislocated,' said James. 'This is going to hurt.' Even as he spoke he took the foot firmly in his grasp, pulled and twisted sharply in one convulsive movement.

Charlotte screamed once, then her eyes rolled in her head and she slipped away into unconsciousness. While she remained comatose they bandaged her ribs, knee and ankle, then gently rubbed a soothing ointment into her multiple lacerations, bumps and bruises. Letty tucked her up in bed, drew the coverlets up to her chin and sat beside her holding her hand consolingly until Charlotte opened her eyes, wincing with pain and beginning to tremble as her memory came flooding back.

'Drink this,' said James, holding out a medicine glass containing a warm brown liquid. Charlotte, too weak to protest, obediently swallowed the mixture, gagging over the taste.

'What is it?' asked Letty.

'An anodyne,' said James. 'Just a few drops of laudanum in hot water. A recommended specific against the ills of the world. In a few moments she will be sleeping like a log.' He stroked away the strands of hair lying across Charlotte's damp forehead.

'Go to sleep, child. When you wake the pain will be gone and we shall be home.'

'And just think,' said Letty, 'what a tale you shall have to tell.'

James smiled at Letty. 'And so shall we, my dear. So shall we.'

Chapter Thirteen

Daniel Fogarty sat alone in the breakfast room of his furnished apartments, sipping at his coffee as he sifted through the morning's post. One letter stood out from among the usual nondescript collection like an aristocrat amid a crowd of beggars. Mystified, he slowly turned it over, examining the expensive texture of the envelope, the London postmark and the heavy black wax seal. Slitting it open he withdrew a sheet of embossed notepaper and read the carefully inscribed curlicues and circumvolutions with a mounting sense of incredulity. Then he rose from the table and began a distracted pacing of the room as his brain tried to grapple with two opposing problems. Eventually, like a man clutching at straws, he opened the door of the glass-fronted bookcase and withdrew his copy of Bradshaw.

He was flicking over the pages, wading through forests of figures and thickets of footnotes, when there was a knock at the door and James strolled in, hands in pockets and a look of insufferable innocence on his face. He cocked an eye at the disarray of breakfast dishes.

' 'Morning,' he announced himself cheerfully. 'Breakfasting late, I see?' He tut-tutted reprovingly. 'You'll never make much headway by rising at this time in the morning. I'm surprised at you, Daniel, by now half the world's work is done.'

'What the devil do you want?' demanded Daniel, irritated at the interruption. He slid the letter between the pages of the Bradshaw and scowled at his visitor.

'I bring good tidings,' said James. He settled uninvited into a chair and helped himself to coffee. 'I have come to give you best.'

'What?' Daniel was in no mood for jocularity.

'I know when I am beaten,' said James with the air of a man who had never known defeat in his life. 'I have sold out. Unloaded my shares. Got out at the top and made a handsome profit, thanks to you. But . . . ' He shrugged. 'You had me caught in a trap. So the company is yours. A sharp piece of business, Daniel. Congratulations.'

'What?' reiterated Daniel mechanically, unable to come to terms with an additional problem.

'The Brazil venture,' James explained patiently. 'Now the company is yours, what do you propose to do with it?'

'Oh, that?' said Daniel abstractedly. He gathered his wits. 'I shall make it pay, of course. And recover my losses. Once the intention is clear the shares will rise again.' He leaned back in his chair and eyed James's innocent features suspiciously. 'I am only surprised you did not put up a harder fight.'

'There comes a time in every game,' said James blandly, 'when it behoves the prudent man to throw in his hand and pick up his winnings.'

Daniel shrugged. 'It is a viable proposition and one which should bring our investors handsome returns. I foresee a great future for Porto Isabella.'

'Port Baines,' James corrected. 'And without a railway it has no future.'

Daniel stared at him. 'What – ?'

'You cannot build the railway,' James explained easily, 'until you have built the bridge. And you cannot build the bridge because I have taken an option on the land on either side of the gorge.' He watched the effect of his words tracing its unmistakable pattern across Daniel's features, steepled his fingers together and smiled benignly. 'Unless we agree to sink our differences and build the port together your shares will not be worth the paper they are written on.'

Daniel's hands felt clammy and unconsciously he rubbed them together. He was a rich man, but there were limits and he had never calculated for a total loss. He would face near ruin. The Yards would come to a standstill. *Elizabeth*, he thought, and remembered the letter sandwiched between the pages of Bradshaw. He made up his mind.

'What are your terms?' he asked thickly.

'Generous,' said James. 'A few Founder's shares, a directorship, and Onedin ships to be afforded the same terms as Frazer ships.'

Daniel frowned. 'But Onedin ships are all sailers,' he objected. 'And you said yourself that it could only be a steamer port.'

'I am looking to the future,' said James. He held out his hand. 'We are agreed, then?'

'In principle,' said Daniel.

'Details,' said James as they shook hands, 'are for lawyers.'

Daniel summoned up a smile. 'And it would seem that marriage is for principals. I understand that congratulations are in order?'

'Thank you,' said James. He grinned ruefully. 'Letty has made a start by turning out the house from top to bottom. It's as busy as an ant heap and reeks of carbolic, while Charlotte is lying abed playing the invalid and enjoying every moment of it. I paid Robert and Sarah a visit to find them in a similar state of turmoil. They are preparing a reception fit for a potentate.'

'O, Lord,' breathed Daniel, and unable to contain himself any longer, imparted his news to James.

James whistled. 'You will go?'

'I must,' said Daniel.

'You will be cutting it mighty fine,' said James.

'I know.' Daniel ran a feverish hand through his hair. 'It's those damned Sailors' Homes. I wish I'd never started them.'

'So you are the philanthropist behind them? Baines conjectured that it must be someone who knew ships and the sea.' James pulled at his nose. 'And now your chickens are coming home to roost with a vengeance.'

Daniel moved across to the sideboard. 'I know it is early

in the morning, but I am in need of a drink. Will you join me?'

'I think it calls for one,' said James. He took the proffered glass of whisky from Daniel. 'As Robert would say, "medicinal purposes".' He took a draught of whisky. 'Now as to practicalities. Are you going to tell Elizabeth?'

Daniel shook his head. 'That is the devil of it, I can't. If I tell Elizabeth, she would be bound to tell Sarah.'

James nodded. 'And that would let the cat out of the bag.' He reflected a few moments while Daniel drained his glass at a gulp and took once again to a purposeless pacing of the room. 'Preparations are afoot and invitations already sent out,' he continued, 'therefore it is too late to put back the wedding. That leaves but one solution: you must take Elizabeth with you.'

'Without giving her a reason?' Daniel shook his head vehemently. 'She would never agree.'

'She will,' said James, 'if she believes that the alternative is to be left waiting at the church.'

'I could never persuade her,' said Daniel. 'Never.'

'Don't try,' advised James. 'Let her persuade you.'

It was easier said than done. Elizabeth flew at him in a passion of rage, her hands opening and closing like talons. 'You have the effrontery to stand there and calmly tell me that you are setting off on a business trip on the eve of our wedding! Business, indeed! What business could be so important that it could not be put back a day or two?'

'It is personal,' said Daniel unhappily.

'Personal!' she screeched. 'More "personal" than your marriage?' She eyed him as though he were a leper. 'Leave now and there will be no marriage!'

'I shall return in time,' he protested weakly.

'From Aberdeen? Aberdeen!' she brayed. 'What possible business could take you to Aberdeen? Aberdeen, of all places!' She choked over the name as though Aberdeen was beyond the civilised pale.

'If it were not imperative I would not dream of going,' he told her haltingly. 'But there is someone I must see.'

'Someone? Who? Just who is this "someone" who is so demanding of your attention that you are prepared to put our happiness to risk at a moment's notice? Does the creature have a name?'

'It is a lady,' he began.

'A lady? Another woman!' Elizabeth's eyes glinted dangerously.

'No, no,' he hastened to reassure her. 'Nothing like that. She is an old lady, and somewhat set in her ways.'

'Old woman, indeed,' snorted Elizabeth. 'She must be a witch to have such a hold over you.'

'It is true that she leaves me little choice,' said Daniel ruefully. 'But I give you my word that I shall be back in good time. I have ordered a private train for the return journey and . . . '

'A *private* train?' Her brows puckered in perplexity. 'It is *that* important to you?'

'It is,' he admitted frankly.

Elizabeth reflected for a moment or two. 'An old lady?' she mused. 'I am overcome with curiosity. Perhaps I should accompany you and see this old Mother Shipton for myself?'

'I wish you would,' he begged earnestly. 'I promise you will not regret it.'

'If I do,' said Elizabeth firmly, '*I* promise that you will rue the day you were born, Daniel Fogarty.'

'I have received a rather strange, and somewhat disturbing communication from Mrs Frazer,' said the Reverend Mr Magnus. 'I wonder if you could perhaps throw a little light on it?'

Robert took the letter, read it through twice, then passed it to Sarah. 'I can't make head nor tail of it. Neither of them ever mentioned the prospect of undertaking such a journey. Certainly not in my hearing.'

'I am sure you will appreciate,' murmured Mr Magnus, wringing his hands, 'that time is of the essence and, in view of the considerable distance involved, I must tell you that I am not sanguine, not sanguine at all.'

Sarah sank back in her chair and fanned the air with the

letter. 'They have eloped!' she wailed. 'I knew it! I knew it in my bones! Oh, the humiliation!'

'Nonsense, Sarah,' said Robert brusquely. 'No one elopes to Aberdeen. Least of all, Elizabeth. Not after she has spent days shopping for her trousseau and being fitted for her wedding dress. Wild horses would not keep her away and she will drag Daniel Fogarty to the altar even if she has to put a ring through his nose.'

'Then I take it that the – ah – arrangements are to go ahead as planned?' questioned Mr Magnus, transferring a hand to his brow.

'Certainly,' said Robert with more confidence than he felt.

'I am relieved to have your assurance,' said Mr Magnus. 'I must admit to harbouring a sense of apprehension on first receiving the intelligence. However . . . ?' Mr Magnus blinked through pale lashes, obviously hoping for a fuller explanation.

'Business,' Robert asserted sententiously, 'can be a demanding taskmaster.'

'Quite, quite,' agreed the unworldly Mr Magnus and allowed himself to be ushered to the door amid Robert's protestations that all would be well.

Robert returned, poured himself a generous tot of medicinal whisky and swallowed it at a gulp. 'My God!' he said. 'If they have left us in the lurch!'

'Oh, spare the thought!' cried Sarah. 'I shall never be able to hold up my head in public again!'

Robert helped himself to a second whisky. 'It's odd,' he said. 'Deuced odd.'

The train snored through the night, its whistle occasionally whimpering in the darkness.

Elizabeth and Daniel had a first class compartment to themselves. It was sumptuously padded with buttoned upholstery, and heavily braided valances hung below the cushioned seats to protect the traveller from unseemly draughts. Elizabeth tucked the travelling rug more firmly about her legs and settled herself comfortably against the corner head-rest. She peeped between lowered lids at Daniel dozing in the opposite corner, arms folded across his chest.

'Don't you think it high time, Daniel, that you told me more of this mysterious errand to Aberdeen?' she asked softly.

He opened his eyes and yawned until his jaws cracked. 'I had intended to wait until we arrived at our final destination – which is not, incidentally, Aberdeen. From there we change to a local and make a short cross-country journey.'

Her eyes widened and she sat bolt-upright. '*Another* change of train? Daniel – we shall never get back in time!'

'We shall,' he assured her.

'But . . . ' She shook her head. 'I don't understand. Where are we going?'

'To Balmoral,' he said. He dipped his hand into his pocket and passed her the embossed sheet of paper. 'This should be explanation enough.'

She took the letter and commenced to read with a frown of concentration which slowly gave way to a look of incredulity. *I am commanded by Her Majesty*, she read, and looked up in disbelief. 'Her Majesty . . . ? The – the Queen . . . ?'

'Read on,' said Daniel smiling.

Elizabeth read the letter through. Then over and over again until the words danced and misted and she began to sob through a mixture of laughter and tears. 'Oh, Daniel!' she wept. 'Oh, dear, dear Daniel . . . !'

The telegram arrived while James and Letty were taking tea with Robert and Sarah.

'What I don't understand,' Robert was saying, 'is Daniel Fogarty's purpose in transforming our old shop into a glorified boarding house.' He wagged his head knowingly. 'He will never make it pay. Never in this world.' Taking the buff-coloured envelope from a silver tray held out by a maid with a cast in one eye, he dismissed her with a curt nod and tore open the cover.

'Oh, my God!' said Robert and sat down heavily.

'What is it?' demanded Sarah. She took one look at Robert's face, mouth opening and closing like a fish agape for air. 'I knew it!' she cried. 'The wretches have eloped! Oh, that scheming little minx! She has planned it, planned it right from the start . . . !'

'No, no,' said Robert waving the telegram. 'It's Daniel. Good grief – I can hardly credit it! He's a "Sir"! I mean, good grief – they have been received by the Queen – the pair of them! Here – read for yourself,' he babbled.

Sarah took the form, commenced to read, then sank slowly back into her chair. 'Letty, dear – my smelling salts, if you please,' she called faintly.

'Brandy for you, Robert?' asked James cheerfully while Letty waved a burnt spill beneath Sarah's nose. He picked up the fallen telegram as Robert gagged over his brandy and Sarah spluttered to her senses. 'I suppose it was always on the cards,' he said. 'What better way to touch the heart-strings of our glorious Monarch than by philanthropic investment in Sailors' Homes, and by further ascribing to them the title of the Prince Albert Foundation?'

Robert peered over the top of his brandy glass. 'You are not trying to tell me,' he demanded thickly, 'that Daniel Fogarty actually planned this?'

'I don't imagine for one moment that he expected a knighthood,' said James. 'He merely cast his bread upon the waters and it has come back liberally spread with butter.'

Sarah leaned forward and clutched Robert's arm. 'Sir Daniel and Lady Fogarty. Lady Fogarty,' she repeated, rolling the words around her tongue. 'Robert – this means that we are allied to the nobility!'

'Not yet,' James reminded her. 'They have first to be married.'

The wedding took place at St Bride's church before all the notables of the city, but not before Elizabeth had kept Daniel, a perspiring Mr Magnus and the entire congregation waiting an unconscionable time while last-minute adjustments were made to her wedding gown.

She entered the church on James's arm as Mrs Frazer and left as Lady Fogarty to the clamour of bells and a snowstorm of confetti.

From the church the cavalcade wound its way to the seclusion of Robert's house where the guests availed themselves of Robert's hospitality and bride and groom retired to change into travelling costume.

Charlotte, perched on a garden swing, sailed pendulum-like between the two boys. Robert, basking in reflected glory, stood teetering gently on his heels at the head of a sweep of steps leading from the lawn to the portico. Sarah scurried from group to group, her shrill voice carrying above the hum of conversation.

'As Lady Fogarty said to me only the other day ...'

'Naturally, I have always been Lady Fogarty's confidante ...'

'I understand that Her Majesty had the kindness to say ...'

'So romantic ...'

'Childhood sweethearts ...'

'Of course Sir Daniel and my husband have always been close, very close ...'

James took Letty's arm and guided her across the lawn as his private carriage, bedecked with ribbons, the horses garlanded with roses, drew up beneath the portico and Daniel and a radiant Elizabeth appeared in the doorway.

'Come along,' he said. 'Let us rescue the happy couple before Sarah can pronounce a benediction.'

The guests, like so many random particles drawn by twin magnets, converged upon the centre of attraction. Robert cleared his throat importantly in preparation for launching into his long-rehearsed impromptu speech. Sarah gathered her prize flock of more important dignitaries about her heels and gushed across, quacking: 'You must permit me to introduce you to my very dear sister-in-law, the Lady Elizabeth ...'

James, Letty laughing and panting behind, broke into a long-legged gallop, headed off Robert and Sarah and quickly bundled Elizabeth and Daniel into the carriage. Daniel reached out a helping hand to Letty and, as James hopped in beside her, the coachman cracked his whip and the equipage rolled away down the driveway and out between the wrought-iron gates and sandstone gateposts.

'Well!' snorted Robert, his speech still clutched in his hand.

'Well!' sniffed Sarah. 'I suppose one cannot make a silk purse out of a sow's ear!'

'Well!' said Daniel, mopping his brow. 'That's a relief! You managed it very well, James. We are obliged to you.'

Elizabeth, flushed and happy, paused to take stock of her surroundings, then eyed James suspiciously. 'Surely this is not the way to the hotel?'

'No,' said James. 'I have a surprise for you. How do you fancy spending your honeymoon cruising the Caribbean?'

'The Carib . . . ? Oh, James – you don't mean it!'

'That is very handsome of you, James,' said Daniel warmly. 'But how . . . ?'

'I have put the *Neptune* at your disposal,' said James. He waved a generous hand. 'She is ready to cast off and put to sea the moment you set foot aboard.'

'Oh, James!' exclaimed Elizabeth, her eyes shining. 'One of your lovely white ships! Oh, you dear, dear romantical man!'

Daniel pumped James by the hand. 'I don't know how to thank you, James!'

'I'll think of something,' said James.

Elizabeth suddenly sat upright. 'My trousseau!' she declared in alarm. 'We must return to the hotel!'

'All is taken care of,' James assured her. 'Baines and a couple of the hands have collected your dunnage. It should be aboard by now.'

The horses cantered along the dock road, swept the carriage between the dock gates and pulled up at the *Neptune*'s gangway.

The ship lay alongside, white and glistening, every line coiled and flaked down, brasswork gleaming in the sun, the blue Onedin flag snapping in the breeze. Baines waited at the head of the gangway, smart in new brass-buttoned uniform with, hovering at his side, the figure of Billy-boy attired in white duck trousers, reefer jacket and a uniform cap falling about his ears.

'Lay aloft!' roared Baines, then stepped forward to beam a greeting to his passengers. 'Welcome aboard, sir and lady.' He rubbed his chin. 'I don't think I'll ever get the hang of it.'

Daniel shook hands. 'You'd best stick to Elizabeth and Daniel,' he said in his broadest Australian accent. 'We don't go for dog on Onedin ships.'

While Letty was taking her leave, James drew Baines to one side and handed him a bulky envelope. 'Your orders, Captain Baines. I expect a fast passage out. And I have a sugar contract to fulfil, so you will load with all speed at Barbados and crack on all sail homeward bound.'

Baines winked broadly. 'The love-birds won't like that.'

James sniffed. 'The *Neptune* is a merchant ship, not a rich man's toy.' He held out a hand. 'A fair wind and a fair passage,' he wished Baines formally, made his farewells to Elizabeth and Daniel, and guided Letty back ashore.

'Let go fore and aft, Mr McArdle,' ordered Baines and took his place on the poop.

James and Letty watched the tug fussing about as it manoeuvred the ship from the quay and, huffing and puffing, paddles thrashing the water, smoke belching from its funnel, towed the *Neptune* through the lock and out into the river.

They continued to watch and wave until the ship spread her white wings and flew down river like a great white bird. Then they made their way back to the waiting carriage.

'You did rather rush them off their feet, James,' mused Letty.

'I couldn't afford to have her miss the tide,' said James. 'Idle ships cost money.'